PRESSURES

OF A

BLACK
MAN

R. M.
BROWN

For contact information, go to:
www.pressuresofablackman.com

Designed by:
Proworks Production, LLC
P. O. Box 7703
Monroe, LA 71211

Printed and edited by:
Rozetta's Graphics
rozetta@sugarlandgraphics.com
409-225-5445

FIRST EDITION

ISBN 978-0-9856297-0-0

*This book is dedicated to
all the men and their families
who have had to suffer abuse just
because of the color of their skin.*

CONTENTS

INTRODUCTION
ACKNOWLEDGEMENTS

ACKNOWLEDGMENTS

To God the Father, Son, and Holy Spirit, through whom all things are possible.

To Gennie B. Byrd, my best friend, who always had my back and taught me to do my best all the time.

To John Byrd, Sr. (late) who always made me laugh and taught me that God is in control all the time.

To Lamica and Krystal Brown for your unconditional love while sharing me with my job and others.

To Harvey Houston for giving me my drive back, believing in me, and pushing me to be that amazing woman he believed in.

To my family and friends for being there for me.

To special friends, Linda Gail (late), Rena, (Lesley Rene) , Ida (late), and Audrey for being there through the process and never judging me.

To Class of 1977, Richwood High School (Go Ram).

PRESSURES OF A BLACK MAN

INTRODUCTION

How does one start a story? When you have no idea, I guess the best place to start is at the beginning. Everyday life and all the problems that come with it can be overwhelming by themselves, but when you factor in the color of your skin, that's when the challenge really comes. *Pressures of a Black Man* is a constant struggle and without our faith in God, the pressures of everyday life would be overwhelming; but being in God's favor is like taking the stress out of our days. Without God in our lives and not being in his favor, some of us could not deal with the day-to-day struggles of everyday living. Just walking down the street, minding your own business, or driving in a car is a constant battle, just because of the color of your skin. We are accused of being lazy. Why do we always have to give 120 percent to prove we are worthy?

This is a story about several Black men who are connected to each other by their up-bringing, environment, and their faith in God. These young black men gave their 120 percent to make a difference by sharing their experiences with other young Black men in their community. They hope that by sharing their experiences of everyday living with these young men, it might help them handle situations of prejudice differently and with less stress. It is not everyday that someone cares about others and their lives and want to make a difference. By giving them the knowledge that it does not have to be this way and that we are in control of our lives, we can make the difference by breaking the cycle. Why keep dong the same thing over? Make a change, break the cycle.

i

CHAPTER 1

CARL JACKSON, JR.

Officer Carl Jackson, Jr. is the first young man we are going to meet. He is an average man who became a police officer because his father was a police officer. Carl Jackson, Sr., his father, was known throughout his community as a good, fair man, who tried to ensure that he made a difference in his community to take some of the pressures off situations, such as police brutality. Carl, Sr. saved a lot of lives, even though police brutality was very common in the community. Because Carl, Sr., a Christian man, was respected by all his fellow officers, he could defuse some of the brutality with his knowledge of the Bible to bring out the humanity of his fellow officers when certain situations were about to become out of control.

Carl, Sr. died in one of those situations. The official story was that he responded to an officer in need of assistance. When he got there, the assailant over-powered him and killed him with his own weapon. The officer he came to assist shot and killed the assailant. This is the official story, not the real story.

Carl, Sr.'s funeral is the reason why Carl, Jr. is a police officer today. The words his mother spoke at his father's funeral were powerful; he never forgot them. She said she understood why her husband became a police officer. She knew that he was in Heaven because everyday he did what he was supposed to, even though he was carrying out man's law, he knew that he was on his job for a reason. Even though her husband was taken away violently, she knew that it was by the grace of God and God does not make mistakes. Sometimes we want to think we are in control of our choices in life, but the only thing that we can be sure of is that God knows the ending and the outcome of everyone's situations. Carl, Sr. had the effect of a rock being tossed across a pond; he had ripple effect on people's lives. She looked at the people attending the funeral and started remembering some of the situations he came across with his fellow officers. She looked lovingly with tears in her eyes at her son, Carl, Jr., and told him that his father worked in the community to try and make a difference in how we as Blacks were being treated by his fellow officers. It was not much, but in some lives, it sometimes meant the difference between life and death.

Carl, Jr. realized that his father had a lot of influence in the community, and also that he wanted to follow in his father's footsteps. He wanted to make a difference in his community because police brutality was still an everyday occurrence. He wanted to take his father's values, which were instilled in him, and try to make a difference in young men's lives who were on the wrong side of the law. He wanted to show them that someone cared and teach them that there is a better life and that they can break the cycle. It is like a mind set "if all you know is hardship and brutality, then that's all you know." Someone once said, "when you know better, you tend to do better."

Carl, Jr. finished high school and went on to get a degree in Criminal Justice. While attending college, he met his soulmate, Cynthia. Cynthia was soft-spoken and she was like his other half. They were so in tuned to each other that one did not have to say that something was wrong for the other one would know without even being told. They had a special bond between them. Cynthia grew up an only child, never knowing who her father was or knowing how having a positive father role model could have a positive impact on her life. She loved hearing stories about Carl, Sr. It made her wish that she had known her father.

The first time Carl, Jr. saw Cynthia, they were at a party. He was watching her from across the room. You could tell she had confidence. She wasn't loud, over-bearing, or uppity. She had a special glow about her. There was a situation going on of which neither Carl, Jr. nor Cynthia were aware. There were some football players who had noticed Cynthia too. She was a beautiful woman, nicely built. She wasn't paying any attention to them. She was enjoying her friends' company. One of the guys walked over to where they were and slipped something into her drink. Carl, Jr., having been watching her from across the room, noticed it and stepped in because he knew something was about to happen that was not right. He became her hero then, her savior, her protector, and has been that ever since. They grew fond of each other overnight. Their friends said that they were joined at the hip, almost inseparable. Cynthia said that he was her savior; he said the same thing about her, she was his safe haven, the person he could talk to about the hardness that went on at work.

CHAPTER 2

OFFICERS TOM HARDIN AND JOHN SMITH

*B*ecause the police department was taking a lot of heat for all the police brutality claims filed against them, for being more brutal towards Blacks, the term "driving while Black" was on the lips of many and an everyday occurrence. It seemed like on a day-to-day basis, there was something happening.

There seemed to be certain ones in the middle of everything. Officers Tom Hardin and John Smith got the majority of the complaints. One would wonder why they were still together as partners, still on the police force, still having a badge and a gun with all the complaints that the police department received on them. These two officers were like night and day. If they were not together, you did not have to wonder who was influencing who.

Sometimes you have to step out on faith when some things are wrong and make them right, regardless of the consequences. Put it all in God's hands and let the chips fall where they may. Officer John Smith was good-natured. He was soft spoken. He always wanted to be a cop. It had always been his dream and now he had his dream. The only thing about his dream that bothered him was being placed with a partner who blamed everything negative that happened to him on Blacks. His home life environment influenced his way of thinking and beliefs. "Nigger" was a constant word in his household. His father was a member of the KKK. Officer Hardin was not a member of the KKK, but with his beliefs and way of thinking, he could have been a cardholder, if they had cards. His beliefs were the same as the KKK.

4

Officer Hardin disliked Blacks so much that every time he heard the complaint on him on "driving while Black," he would laugh. He made sure that he never crossed the line. He would walk up to the line, toy with it by touching it, but he knew better than to cross it. Everyday on the job that line was touched and after a while, it would not be controllable. The day would come when Hardin and Smith would cross that line.

CHAPTER 3

SMOOTH

There was a young Black man driving in a pimped out old school car with the rims and King Kong speaker in his trunk. He was just driving along, minding his own business, but he fit the stereo-type of being a drug dealer or thug. Even being Black, we stereo-type these young men too without finding out the truth. This time, the circumstances just happened to be true. The young man just happened not to be riding dirty at the time. This young man had the smart-mouth and flip attitude that these white cops could not do anything because he worked for Captain.

Sometimes we can defuse a situation by just saying yes or no, without all the attitude, just to make sure we get out of a situation safely with as little confrontation as possible with authority. This young man was "Smooth." He was called Smooth because of his demeanor. He was a smooth talker, nicely dressed in hip-hop fashion - everything matching from head to toe; the baseball cap, throw-back jersey, jeans, and name brand tennis shoes.

Smooth was Captain's second in command. Captain was top dog; he ran the block. Everything dealing with drugs came through him. Captain was smart. He was so smart that he had his system set-up so if anything went down, it could not be traced back to him. Captain was not an ordinary drug dealer who was slinging drugs because he had to or needed to. Captain's family was very well off. He grew up in a household where everything that was wanted was provided. Captain got in the drug scene because he could. It gave him the feeling of being needed and wanted. Because his family worked hard to ensure the family's needs were well provided, there was little time to give them the attention and love that children needed when they are growing up. His drug empire gave him the feeling of being needed and loved.

On this particular day, Smooth was just hanging out, riding and enjoying his music. With Smooth's luck, he just happened to ride by Officers Hardin and Smith. Knowing who they were, he knew he was good, because he was clean and had nothing to fear. They pulled him over, ran his tags, and realized that he was Captain's right hand. Hardin used this opportunity to try get some information on Captain so he could enhance his promotion position with the department. Smooth, looking through his rear-view mirror, laughed because he knew they did not have anything on him. He was driving the speed limit and had no drugs on him this time. Both Smith and Hardin got out of the patrol car. Hardin, walked up the driver's side; Smith was behind the car.

Officer Hardin asked Smooth, "where is the fire?"

Smooth asked, "what do you mean. I was driving the speed limit."

Hardin said, "you were speeding, so where is the fire? With Captain?"

At that moment, Smooth realized that they had another motive when they stopped him. Smooth said, "No man, I wasn't speeding. Your radar got to be wrong officer," real sarcastic.

Hardin said, "Step out of the car."

Smooth asked, "why, so you can beat me?"

Officer Hardin again said, "exit the car."

Officer Smith realized that this situation was about to get out of control. He walked up between them. "I need to see your driver's license, vehicle registration, and proof of insurance," he said to Smooth.

Smooth said something else smart, "Oh, now we're going to play good cop, bad cop."

Officer Smith's attitude changed toward Smooth then and he felt that whatever Hardin does to him, he deserves.

Smooth, reached for the items asked for out of his glove compartment, saying "I'm tired of all the harassment by you f--king cops. Why can't we wear nice clothes, drive nice cars without all this drama from y'all? This s--t ain't what it do." He threw the license, vehicle registration and proof of insurance at Hardin.

At that moment, Officer Hardin opened the door and pulled Smooth out of the vehicle and threw him up against the vehicle, saying "I guess I be bad cop" with a sarcastic sneer in his voice. He then took his night stick and punched Smooth in his ribs twice.

Smooth, catching his breath, said "Wait till Captain hears about this."

Hardin then said, "Then let's really give you something to tell." He then took his baton and hits Smooth across the face. "Now tell him we're coming to get him, and you know what, you are going to help us with that whether you want to or not."

Smooth jerked away from Hardin and said, "You're f--king nuts, thinking I'm going to help you. That's like signing my death warrant."

Hardin said, "if you don't, he's going to think you are and since I'm the bad cop, I'm going to make sure he thinks you are anyway. You know we can make it look like you are and I don't think Captain will be too happy with you."

Smooth knew this was true. Several of his boys had been setup by the cops and they came up missing. No one knew what happened to them; if were dead or if they left town. Because the cops had them set up to take the falls for them because they wouldn't help them in their investigations by being their snitch. Smooth knew that he was caught between a rock and a hard place. It was a no win situation for him. So he decided to give them what they wanted and prayed that he had enough time to get out of town before Captain found out about it. If he didn't tell them what they wanted, he would be killed because they were going to make sure Captain thought he was feeding them information.

Smooth's mind went back to all he wanted to do today was go for a ride and listen to his music, and now his whole life had taken another turn. He was thinking "God how am I going to get out of this." Not realizing that God was the answer and the only answer.

When they released him, he went home. His mother and father were at home and they were astonished by all the bruises on their son. Smooth told them, "I was out riding and was stopped by some cops and they did this to me."

His father grabbed the telephone to call the police, but Smooth yelled at him, "No, I'm in enough trouble as it is."

His father yelled, "I knew you were going to get yourself into a spot you wouldn't be able to get yourself out of while hanging out with those friends of yours."

His mother was crying because she could tell he was hurt badly. Even though he didn't want to go to the hospital, he knew he was hurt badly, so he agreed to go.

While they were at the hospital, his father, going against Smooth's wishes, called the police and told them what his son had told them. They also called the local Black newspaper and Black activists in the community. Because the community (Black) in particular was in constant struggle with the police department with all the police brutality, the local activists wanted everything publicized to get all the publicity they could get to show that police brutality was a major problem in the community.

Because police brutality was such a major problem, some of the local activists got together with a young Black attorney who had an idea on how they could try and get a handle on this problem through education. They formed a non-profit organization called "Pressures of a Black Man" (POABM). POABM was formed to educate young Black men on everyday problems that are common in their lives, and to teach them ways to handle these problems in a positive manner.

CHAPTER 4

STEVEN YOUNG

P ressures of a Black Man" was founded by Steven Young. He and Carl, Jr. were classmates in high school and are still friends. Steven grew up in a different type of household than Carl, Jr. He grew up in a single parent household with his mother, Gloria Young. Steven was extremely intelligent. His IQ was that of a genius. He was the first one in his family to go to college. His mother was so proud of him she made sure that he got a good education. Steven was an unselfish child, always giving. The love of his mother influenced him and this is one of the main reasons why he started the Center for young Black men, to let everyone know that we can make a difference and to give of ourselves when God gives to us.

Steven believed he should be able to give back to others unselfishly to ensure someone else has a chance of making a better life for themselves. Steven formed this organization after he started practicing law and realized there was a need for it. Even though police brutality was rampant, Steven realized that we can make a situation worse by our attitude. Another reason for starting POABM was to educate young Black men that we have to be bigger and better than the abusive policemen. And then if we catch them at fault and they can't point a finger at us, we stand a better chance of ensuring we can make a change when we go to court.

Sometimes our attitude can really influence how the police re-acts toward us and that is one of the reasons why we are always being caught up in situations. Always being blamed for things like they are on automatic; that someone Black did it. Like

11

assuming just because we are walking down the same street as someone White, we are up to no good because they are quick to stereotype. Change our attitude and demeanor may change certain situations when it comes to the police department. If we take out our attitude, then what else can they blame on us?

Steven wanted this organization to be like Big Brother, but only dealing with the problems that occurred in the life of Black men. The issue of growing up in a single parent household, driving while Black, stereotyped by the way we dress as a drug dealer or thug, not being able to get jobs or promotions, being blamed for everything that goes wrong, the problem with affirmative action, and our voting rights. Some of these issues are in other races, but he only wanted to deal with the problems in the Black community at that time, but knew there would be crossover into other races later on. He also wanted to teach them that if they want to get into college, it doesn't start in Jr. High, it starts in elementary school, in the preschool and first grade.

He wanted to help them deal with day-to-day issues when they walk out their door. There is a chance they can be wrongly accused of a crime because of their skin color. The right to vote is their right. Our forefathers fought for that right so that our voting voice could mean something. The voice of anyone or any ethnic group means something when they come together for a cause.

Steven wasn't married. He was a work-alcoholic, devoted to his job and making sure that his mother was well provided for. Because of all the sacrifices she made to give him a good education, he made sure she had everything she needed. He was a good and loving son, and thanked God daily for his mother, because without her, he would not be the Steven Young he is today. Steven's mother and Smooth's mother were good friends. They had worked together and went to the same Church and fellowship a lot together. When Smooth's mother asked Steven's mother to ask him if he would take on Smooth's case with the police, she told her that she would relay the message to Steven, but she didn't get involved in his law practice. She definitely would make sure he would give them a call and if there was anything he could do, he would do it or tell them where to go.

CHAPTER 5

STEVEN AND SMOOTH

*S*teven took on Smooth's case and one of the things he asked Smooth initially was "What did you do to stop this situation from happening."

Smooth looked at Steven like he didn't understand and said, "What are you saying, what did I do to stop the situation?"

Steven asked the question again. "Did you say or do anything to make them mad?"

Smooth said on the defensive, "I wasn't doing anything wrong. I was just driving and they stopped me, wanting to know about a friend of mine, Captain, and then they threatened me to help them get Captain, saying if I didn't go along, they would make sure Captain thought that I did."

Steven realized that Smooth was hooked up with one of the most notorious drug dealers in the city. Steven thinks that maybe he had agreed to something he could not deliver. Even though he never had a client like Smooth before, he knew that regardless of what he thought about what Smooth did at that time, he knew he had to take his case on because the police brutality claim was worse and maybe he could have some influence on Smooth.

Smooth told Steven, "I wasn't doing anything wrong, but I'm not saying that I was no angel either. But this time, I'm innocent. In order for them to have a chance at getting Captain, they had to intimidate and threaten me to make sure I was a part of their sting operation against Captain. Officer Hardin made sure I knew that if I didn't cooperate with them, they would make sure Captain thought I was a snitch."

14

Steven looked at Smooth and said, "I' going to ask you one more time. What did you do to stop this situation from happening? When they gave you the attitude, did you give them attitude back?"

Smooth said, "Hell yea. Why wouldn't I? Them m--rf--kers stopped me for no reason, beat me, and threatened me with leaking information so that Captain would think I'm a f--king snitch to get me killed. Man, f--k them. Those m-----rf--kers better be glad I wasn't strapped or there would be two dead cops today. They only f--king with me because they can. Those m---rf--kers got me in a jam. I'm f--ked either way it go down. All I wanted to do is get out of this s--t breathing. If I do, then I'm gone. All I want is a second chance."

Steven didn't believe Smooth wanted a second chance to make amends, but just to get out of the situation, on the other hand he thought he was being judgmental so he could go back to life as usual.

Steven said, "This is what we are going to do. I run a Center called Pressures of a Black Man. I want you to join so when we go to court, we can let the judge see you're trying to make a change in your life by helping other people."

Smooth said, "Man, that ain't what it do. I don't need to help anybody. Nobody helped me."

Steven tried to explain to Smooth that he would be helping his own case by volunteering at the Center. By sharing his experience of police brutality with other young Black men, he could teach them how to interact with the police so that they can change how the police interact with the Black citizens on routine stops. Also he could teach them how to get their claims for police brutality to stick when the police were crossing the line and they were caught so the case could stand a better chance in court. By remaining calm and answering without the attitude, the police would have nothing to use against them. The ones that don't care about how they treat people will be off the chain regardless of our behavior and we can get them fired.

Steve knew how he was going to defend Smooth because he was accustomed to handling cases where young Black men had attitudes against the cops because of the way they were treated when stopped. This is one of the reasons why he started the organization, to make sure that the charges of police brutality stick when they went to court.

Steven decided that one of the things he was going to do was use some of his influence with high ranking Black officials to see if he could get a liaison between the Black community and the police department. The first person who came to mind was his childhood friend, Carl Jackson, Jr. When Steven and the committee met, he recommended Carl, Jr. giving a great background presentation on him and his father Carl, Sr.'s involvement in the community. The committee voted unanimously to have Carl, Jr. as the Liaison between the police department and the community. The Police Commissioner was invited to the meeting and agreed that this was something that was needed in the community and was glad he was invited.

CHAPTER 6

CARL JACKSON, JR.'S NEW JOB

*T*he Commissioner went to Carl, Jr.'s Captain and explained what was going to happen if Jackson accepted the new job position. The Captain called Carl, Jr. into his office. Carl, Jr. had no idea why he had to report to the Captain's office. He could not think of anything he had done wrong. None of his fellow officers knew. Everyone had their ideas but no one knew what was really going on. His record was spotless. He wasn't up for promotion. When you know nothing, you assume the worst. When he entered the Captain's office, his curiosity ran wild, especially when he saw that the Police Commissioner was there too.

His Captain said, "take a seat."

After shaking hands with them, he took a seat. The Commissioner explained that, "the police department has an above average number of police brutality cases, and that most of the complaints were dealing with Black citizens. Some local Black citizens have formed an organization that is partnering with the police department and the Black community. The young man over the Center is a childhood friend of yours, Steven Young, and he recommended you for the position of liaison between the Black community and the police department. This is not a front or a whitewash, this is something that is very much needed and will show good faith on our part. We need to get these renegades out of the department. We want the community to know that we don't condone this behavior."

Carl, Jr. said, "I am flattered that you considered me, but I prefer to stay where I am."

The Commissioner stood up and said, "we know you're a good cop and that you're good at what you do, but I see the same potential in you that I saw in your father. Carl, Sr., did a lot of good work on the streets. We worked on the streets at the same time and back then he was someone of whom to be proud. This was his number one cause and I think he would want you to at least think about it. Talk it over with your wife before you give us your final decision."

Carl, Jr. asked, "when do you need an answer."

The Commissioner said, " yesterday. We need to change the public's opinion of the department. To show we are taking a stand against brutality and holding the ones responsible account-able through disciplinary actions and discharging them to ensure that they cannot apply for a department job in law enforcement and start all over again somewhere else. We need to be involved with the community, showing a positive side of the department. In every area of life, there are some bad apples. If left unchecked and we don't remove them, they can spoil the whole batch."

Carl, Jr. nodding his head said, "you're right, but I don't make this big of a decision on the spur of the moment or on my own. I do need to consult with my wife and will give you an an-swer soon."

Carl, Jr., walked out of the Captain's office with mixed emotions. His father's death came back to him, how he died trying to help the community and then he could hear his father's voice talking to his friends about the brutality going on in the community, even though he was doing all he could, there was still a lot more that could be done.

After Cynthia heard about what the new job entailed, she told her husband, "you need to pray and leave it in God's hands. Whatever your decision, I will be behind you. I know you want to be involved in the community like your father did. Maybe

God is trying to tell you something. This may be your time to make a change."

She looked at him and said smiling, "Put it in God's hands." She then walked up to him and gave him a big hug.

Carl, Jr. hugging his wife says, "I knew you were going to say that."

She smiled looking back at him and teased him saying, "come on, you know we got that connection."

This was the start of Carl, Jr. becoming the liaison between the Black community and the police department.

CHAPTER 7

JAMES BENTON

*J*ames Benton is another Black man who became a part of Pressures of a Black Man to share his experiences. James was an Assistant Store manager for Lee's Outdoor Paradise. He started working for Lee's Outdoor Paradise right out of high school. It was his first job. He grew up around hunters and fishermen and knew all the things they went through. It came natural to relate to the customers even though the majority of the customers were White. They tended to always ask for him because he always went out of his way to accommodate them. This gave him the edge over his peers. If there was something they wanted and Lee did not have it or did not carry it at that time, James made sure the store looked into getting the items in the future and where they could get it at that time. He made a habit of knowing his customers personally, calling them by their first name or saying Mr. So and So, depending on how they interacted with him. James worked hard to be promoted to the position of Assistant Store Manager. He was an over-achiever, but still prided himself on being a good father, husband, and very involved in his church. The only thing that James was not involved in was his community affairs.

The ratio of Blacks who worked for Lee's Outdoor Paradise was not enough to even make a percentage on a graph. Being an Assistant Store Manager was almost unheard of. This was an accomplishment by itself of which he could be proud. Some would say it was being in the right place at the right time. James believed that it was God's will because how often would a Black man be put in his position and still make a difference?

One of the people whom James thanked God for putting in his life was Mr. Johnny Jones. Mr. Jones was the Store Manager who gave James his chance to make a difference. Mr. Jones was an average White man with average White views. The only difference was he grew up poor and struggled to get where he was. One of his values was that the people who worked for him would do what they were supposed to all the time which made a big impression on him. James had those characteristics and more. He did work that was not his and also ensured that everything that was in his job position was done. Mr. Jones, being a Christian man, rewarded James even with all the heat that he got when he promoted him.

Mr. Jones had not been feeling well lately. James asked him about it. He laughed and said it was just old age creeping up on him. "You know when you get older, you just can't do some of the things you use to," he said.

Early one morning, James got a phone call from Mr. Jones' wife saying she had to rush him to the hospital. He wanted him to go and take over the store until they could find out what was wrong. She had left a message with the corporate office also. James was in "shock" and nervous about the whole situation, but he was confident that he could handle the job. His nervousness came from not wanting to let Mr. Jones down while he was ill. The corporate office called the store and officially told James he was in charge until Mr. Jones came back. After getting the phone call, James said a prayer for the Lord to guide him and show him what he needed to do to make sure everything stay in line until Mr. Jones was able to return to work. James could not wait to go home to tell his wife that it was official - that he was in charge until Mr. Jones returned.

While at work that same day, James got a phone call from Mr. Jones' wife stating his illness was more serious than they first

21

thought. He was going to be out for a good while, that there was no definite date as to when he could return to work. Mr. Jones had been diagnosed with prostate cancer and it was not in the early stages of the disease. James took the news as if someone had stepped on his chest and cut off his air supply. He never thought it was that serious, thinking it was just as he said, old age getting the best of him. Now, along with being in charge until Mr. Jones returned, he had to think about what if he's not able to return. Then the possibility of him being in charge of his own store brought mixed emotions to him. He thought about it but never thought it was something that was attainable because Mr. Jones was not going anywhere. This made him think about how life can change in a split second.

"That's why we should be conscience of our lives if we're in tune with God because you never know when its your time to meet our Maker," James thought.

James knew that there was a serious possibility that the store could really be his. There was not a Black Store Manager and very few Assistant Store Managers with Lee's Outdoor Paradise. He knew his work record and ethics were above average. They spoke for themselves. The company was big on family values and community involvement. The only involvement James had was his involvement in his Church. Other than that, he didn't have any other outside activities going on.

He remembered watching the news and they were having a Ribbon Cutting Ceremony for a new Center and he knew both the guys, Steven and Carl, Jr., from school. This could be his opportunity to become more involved in the community. James took over the store and took it to new heights, breaking sales records. What James did was trained the employees on some of his salesmanship strategies such as getting to know the customers by name, always trying to make sure to meet their needs, making them feel at home. Instead of him knowing all the customers, the whole staff knew everyone. Now, he had everyone on the same page and sales were increasing. Everybody was still worried about Mr. Jones, but was glad James was the one in charge of the store. James did not know it, but Mr. Jones also knew that James, with his outgoing personality, was one of the main reasons why the store was one of the top five stores in the company and one of the reasons why he promoted him to Assistant Manager. Unbeknownst to James, the store's atmosphere and employees' attitude changes made the customers feel like they were talking to a friend. If they did not know the customer's name, he encouraged them to learn it by asking, reading names on their clothes, and looking at their check. If a customer was within five feet or if they made eye contact with them, they were to acknowledge them. They were to always ask if they found everything they needed, and if they had a special order, to tell them when it was coming in, and ensure that they, the employee, would continue to check on the order to make sure there were no delays. Always making the customer feel at home. Now, instead of just James, his whole team were James' and the customers were telling their friends. Word of mouth made sales take off.

James was so proud of the workers and everything that was happening. When he went to visit Mr. Jones, he couldn't wait to tell him.

Mr. Jones smiled and told him, "I never doubted you. I'm going to tell you first, corporate doesn't know it yet. I'll be calling them tomorrow to tell them that I won't be coming back to work and I'm going to recommend that they give you the store."

James' heart was filled with mixed emotions, joy and pain. Joy because he was being given a rare opportunity and pain because he was losing a very dear friend, even though they were of different ethnic groups. Because he gave him a chance when

23

others would not.

Mr. Jones said, "I am recommending you, but it will be up to corporate to make the final decision. I've been gone for six months and out of the circle. All the reports that I have seen have been good, nothing negative, so I'm assuming everything is okay. But you know how corporate America is sometimes. You think everything is okay and they can blind-side you. I will be calling corporate and promise you my recommendation as the next Store Manager."

James was overwhelmed with emotions. He could hardly breath from the excitement. He went home and told his wife what Mr. Jones had said. She was excited for him. She was his backbone. She kept him grounded when things got rough.

She was a Christian too and she told him, "God is the head of our house and we are not going to count our eggs before they hatch. Everything God has in store for us will fall into place."

She was a firm believer in what the song said, "What God has for me," and told him that "if God meant this for you, James, it will be and if you don't get the store, just think of what God is going to bless us with."

James looked at her and wondered why she was saying this when he had taken the store to a new level. He said, "There is no reason why corporate shouldn't give me the store. I've sat sales records in the last six months up 40 percent, and this is something that was unknown until now."

His wife looked at him again and said, "the devil is always around being busy. We're just going to let God's will be. We're going to go with the flow whatever happens, happens. I just don't want you to set yourself up for failure. I'm here for you regardless."

James got a message from the corporate office the next

day, stating that Mr. Jones was not coming back, and that he was still in charge of the store until further notice. There would be no immediate change but within the next two weeks, a new Store Manager would be announced. James didn't like the sound of the message. He replayed it over and over, trying to read into it. His faith was shaken for a minute because he thought he was doing everything he was supposed to do and then for this to be happening is a test of his faith. He called his wife and played the message to her.

She said to him, "let's pray," and at the end of the prayer, she said, "Lord, let your will be done in your son Jesus name, we pray."

After that, James felt like a weight had been lifted off his shoulders. He realized that God was in control of their lives. Sometimes our wants get in the way of our needs. His thinking changed to maybe this is something he didn't need at the time. He went to work every day with a new outlook.

He learned two weeks into the month that corporate would be in the next week. He told everyone that they would be having visitors from the corporate office. The store was already in line; just needed some extra attention to cosmetic details.

When the corporate team came in, they brought a new Store Manager, a White man. James was taken back a little. They gave him the new Store Manager history during the whole process. James was in constant prayer especially when they asked him to train him. He could not believe they asked him to train this young man, after all he had done for the store and with the team of employees.

After talking with the new Store Manager, he realized that he was a shareholder's son. That the only reason he did not get the promotion was because of who you know. He then thought to himself that it has always been who you know. The

25

employees were quite upset with the decision also, but James led the example, keeping a positive attitude and praying.

He told the employees, "we are not in charge of our destiny and if we were in charge, some of us wouldn't be here. We have to be adaptable to change, go with the flow until you own your own business or in a position where you cam make the changes that you feel are right. My personal feelings on me not getting the promotion will not pay my bills or feed my family and support them. Our new boss is not from here, but guess what, we're still going to work for him everyday."

The employees could tell that James was hurt because everyone also thought that James would get the position. He should have gotten the position, but its like he said, "It's not up to us. Sometimes, it is not always what we want, but what we need at that time."

James left work that day. He had not called his wife. He wanted to tell her in person because he needed her strength right now. When he got home, she had a beautiful dinner prepared for him with family and friends. Instead of congratulations on your promotion party, she switched it because someone had called her and told her he did not get the position. She made it a "He's a jolly good fellow and we love you party." Everyone came out to show their love and support and that they believed in him and that he was going to be alright.

James realized at that time that it was going to be alright and his faith got a whole lot stronger. No matter what happens in his life, he could get through it with God on his side. He realized that this was small stuff because he still had a job, a family who loved him, and still had the Lord in his life and he was well loved.

After everyone had left and he was sitting in his chair, his wife came around in front of him and knelt down and put his

26

hand in hers and she started to pray and when she finished praying, she said to him, "everything Is going to be alright. God is watching over us."

James looked at her and said, "you know that I know this is true but then the human side really wants to be mad as hell. But I'm not going to get mad. I'm going to go to work everyday and do my job. If I didn't get anything else out of this, I learned you can't assume you're going to get something because its right. You still have to wait and see what the outcome is going to be. This made me understand that I need to stay with the Center and the reason why is because I can soften the blow for those young men who are going to be in the same situation I'm in and some of them are not going to handle it as well as I have. To make sure they understand, even though they're not saying it's my skin tone, who knows what their reasoning was and maybe God has something bigger and better ahead for me. So, I'm telling you baby, I'm still going to be working and be involved in the Center. I want to thank you for having my back."

James and his wife sat there holding each other. Neither one said anything - both thinking along the same lines - "it was going to be alright, but it was going to take some time to get used to the situation." They knew that God was on their side and they were in his favor and all they had to do was leave it with him.

CHAPTER 8

SEAN MOORE/CAPTAIN

Sean Moore grew up in a family that made a lot of sacrifices to ensure that all the needs of the family were provided. They were good Christian people who had been blessed by God with wealth and they knew it. They always acknowledge that God was the reason why they were successful.

Sometimes people looked down on them because they had money. It was like the saying goes, "How can you judge a book by its cover if you haven't read it?" Sean's parents were very loving and giving parents to their children and their community. Because they were blessed, they blessed others by giving back. Sean's sister was a shy person, not outgoing. Sean was the one who took on all those outgoing qualities, the one who always wanted to be the center of attention. Sean's parents, because of their job responsibilities, didn't spent a lot of quality time with them. That is one of the reasons why Sean lead a double life. He was the good and loving son, and then he was Captain, the drug kingpin who ran his empire on fear.

When Sean was around his parents or their friends, he was the center of attention, always well spoken. Everyone always thought he was the perfect son. A lot of the people did not know Sean's other side, Captain. He had always tried to ensure that he kept Captain on the down-low from his family and their friends. The few that met him in his alter ego of Captain knew by word of mouth the reputation that if they were to say or leak to anyone that Captain was Sean Moore, the son of Edward Moore and Moore & Moore Manufacturer, that it was not going to be pretty. People had been known to disappear when they crossed Captain.

There was no way to prove Captain had anything to do with it. The evidence was always circumstantial. Captain, on the other hand, was mostly mild-mannered, joking at times, but everyone knew that he was strictly about his business. Never leaving anything to chance. His father's business quality came out in him and he used those qualities to run his empire. Captain was set up to be out of harm's way when it came to his business. There was never no way to connect him to anything because he never picked up or took any drugs anywhere. Drugs were never in his presence. Captain was not a user. Captain came on the drug scene not because he was trying to make a better life for himself, but one would think because it gave him that God-like complex. Actually, due to the lack of attention from his parents while he was growing up, all he wanted was a feeling of being loved and needed and that's how he felt when he was Captain. His parents were over-achievers and wanted to leave Sean and his sister a legacy to carry on.

Captain held this against his family. He would have given anything for some of their time; to have his father and mother come to some of his games like his friends' parents. This is why he was who he was today.

Captain ran his block like a business. It almost ran itself. One would think that the fear factor was a good reason why everything ran so smooth. As stated before, people did come up missing. No one knows if they are floating somewhere, buried somewhere, or if they just left town to get away from it all. Assumptions were made. Everyone assumed that they were all dead.

Captain was worried about Smooth because he was acting strange since he had the run-in with the cops and they had beaten him up. Captain asked him, "Do you want something done about it."

Smooth said, "No, I just want to leave well enough along because it only makes matters worse."

Captain asked again, "you're sure?"

Smooth said, "I'm sure man, I just want it to be over with. I'm going to change cars, that way I can be on the down low."

Captain said, "sure but whose going to pull your load if you're on the down low?"

Smooth realized that he said the wrong thing and tried to correct it by saying "I'm not saying someone going to be doing my job. I'm just not going to be out and about on my time. My mom is worried about the cops pulling a kick door sting. I keep trying to tell her that its going to be alright."

Sean asked, "why do you think they want to do a kick door at your home? You're not dumb enough to take products home are you?"

Smooth said, "No man, you know that ain't what it do. But who knows what those cops are thinking? I'm just going to wait until everything quiet down and the lawyer gets everything squared away."

Captain asked, "Are you bringing heat down on us.

Smooth said, "I don't know, I don't know what's going on."

"Why did you go to the cops in the first place?" Captain said.

"Smooth stated, "it wasn't me, it was my parents. You know how they are."

Captain said, "yeah man, I know they're good and loving and always caring."

His eyes told another story though like there was a different meaning to them. And Smooth wondered what made that look come over him.

Captain said, "It's not everyday parents care about your

well-being and not try to make it alright with money. It's good that your parents love you enough to ensure that those cops get what they deserve. If it had been my parents, they would have paid someone to make sure they didn't have a job, instead of seeing that they were punished for it."

CHAPTER 9

WILLIS HEARNE

*A*t that time, Captain decided to take a ride to clear up some thoughts about his parents and Smooth's strange behavior. He always kept a low profile. He made sure he was not caught up in the stereotype of a drug kingpin. His mannerism and demeanor had never been flamboyant, even where he lived, the car he drove, and his style of clothes. While driving, Captain decided to stop and browse for a present for his sister's birthday at one of the local stores. While browsing, he ran across a high school classmate, Willis Hearne. He had not seen Willis since graduation.

Willis was a basketball icon when they were in high school. He was ranked one of the top high school players in their time. He was scouted by all the major universities. Everyone wanted to sign him. But Willis' life took a different turn and the reason why was that he was very much in love with his high school sweetheart, Sonya. Willis and Sonya knew that they were going to get married. One day, they started having sex without protection, their first time. Even though it was their first time, they decided to practice safe sex after that, but it was too late. As the saying goes, "it only takes one time."

Willis' father was never there for him, even though he lived in the same household. His father was never around, always gone and when he was home, he made their lives miserable. He was not a loving husband or father. Willis wanted to be there for his child, so after graduation, he did the honorable thing, he married Sonya and got a job at one of the local companies, Moore and Moore Manufacturer.

Captain went over to speak to Willis, "Hey man, how have you been doing? What's been up?"

Willis turned to see who was talking to him and realized that it was Sean, his old high school buddy. He said, "Hey man, long time no see. I don't think I've seen you since high school. What's you been up to?"

Captain said, "nothing, just a little this and that. What's been up with you and how is Sonya doing? I haven't seen her since high school either."

There was a sad expression that came over Willis' face. Willis explained to Sean that, "Sonya died six months ago of breast cancer and now I'm just trying to take care of everyday one day at a time. We have two daughters and I'm taking care of them. It's been hard because we were so connected and did everything as a unit. It's still hard to believe that she is gone. She took care of a lot of the financial matters for the family. I made sure all the cars and household matters were taken care of but she was our backbone, a good decent woman. She was the glue that held us all together. Now, we're trying to go on without her. The girls are having a hard time; I'm having a hard time dealing with the loneliness. I just want my wife back, but I know that's impossible."

Sean looked at Willis and asked, "Is there anything I can do."

Willis said, "no, unless you can talk your dad into giving me a big raise."

Sean looked at him and said, "well, you know I don't deal with them at the company. I just do a little side work."

Willis asked, " Is there was anything in your side work that I can do until I get back on my feet, because instead of two incomes in the family, there's only one now. The insurance money went to a lot of medical bills."

33

Sean said, "I don't think you want to do the side work I do with you having a family and all, because its kind of complicated."

Willis looked at Sean and said, "Captain, I think I can handle it."

Sean smiled at Willis and said, "if you hadn't said it, I wasn't going to because I keep my personal and business lives separate and my business affairs are not something I broadcast."

Willis told Captain, I need some help; this is not something I want to do for the rest of my life, just until I can get back on my feet."

Sean looked at Willis and said, "I don't normally do this, but because it's you man, I'm going to help you. Meet me tomorrow, okay?"

They exchanged phone numbers and then went their separate ways. Willis went to pick up his daughters and Sean went back to the house where everybody was hanging out.

CHAPTER 10

CAPTAIN BREAKS HIS RULE

S mooth is still there.

Sean asked Smooth, "go and pick up the package from West 34th."

Smooth is really confused now and asks Sean, "are you asking me to bring the package up for you personally."

Sean said, "yes, you got a problem with that?"

Smooth said, "no, I'm just not getting it. You don't handle any of the products, your rule. Why all of a sudden things change?..."

Smooth stopped in mid-sentence because Captain had that look about him, like who are you to question me.

Smooth then said, "okay," and left.

While sitting in his car, Smooth knew that this would probably be his only opportunity to turn Captain in and prayed that there would be enough time for him to get out of town before Captain realized that it was him who turned him in. Smooth had a sleepless night because he had called Hardin and told him that Captain would have a package on him the next day. The next day, Captain got the package from Smooth.

Smooth asked, "Are you sure about this?"

Captain turned and said, "see you later."

Smooth left knowing that this probably would be his last time seeing Sean. He then made the phone call to Hardin, telling him that he delivered the package to Captain.

Officer Hardin said "I thought you said Captain never handled anything personally. If this is a set-up, you're going to regret it."

Smooth said, "this is not a set-up. This is on the up and up. He has a package with him now at the house. This is no hoax. I don't know what he's going to do with it, and no, he doesn't normally handle them as a rule." Then Smooth hung up.

Hardin called the Police Captain of his precinct and said, "I just got a tip on Captain and then explained."

The Police Captain asked, "how reliable is your source. One of the reasons Captain has stayed so clean is that we have never been able to connect him with any drugs, either on him or in his presence."

Hardin said. "the tip is reliable."

Hardin and Smith picked up the search warrant for the house at the address Smooth gave them, and called for backup. They staked out the house waiting until they saw Captain before they used the search warrant.

Captain called Willis and said, "meet him at the house" and gave him the address. Willis showed up and Captain let him in.

Hardin and Smith thought they had just hit the jackpot.

Captain told Willis, " if you deliver this package without any problem, there will be five grand in it for you when you get back. I will make a phone call and if everything is okay, then we will do this once a month until you get straightened out and back on your feet. I don't normally do this, but we go way back and like you said, just until you get back on your feet."

Willis told Captain, "You don't know how much I appreciate this." He then looked at Captain and asked "why?."

Captain asked, "what do you mean, why?"

Willis said again, "why are you doing this?"

Captain stated, "because you are a friend of mine from the old days. Besides, I like you and you have always been good people.

"No man", Willis said, "why are you out here dealing drugs? You and I both know that you don't have to do this."

Captain laughed and said, "you know I don't know the answer to that. Because you're right, I never wanted for anything. I could have a job with my father's company. I just can't answer that man. Only thing I guess I can say is I need to feel needed and wanted. My mother and father were always working, never thinking about us getting the love and affection that we deserved. We were spoiled by them. If they missed something or felt guilty about something, they brought gifts or gave money. I think it was too easy for me to get into the drug scene because I didn't have to. I guess this is my way of defying my parents. Who knows, one day I might wake up and get out of the game and then who knows, only God knows. He could take me out of this game all together. You wouldn't think God plays a major part in my life because of what I do, but he does. Because if I wasn't suppose to be here now, I wouldn't be. What we're doing today is out of the ordinary for me and also for you. I remember you and your wife and everything you gave up for your family. And I think that another reason why I'm helping you is because you lived the life I wished my family had lived. It's got to be God because its surely not me."

Willis was stunned because he never thought someone dealing drugs would be thinking about God. "You know what, I never thought about it that way. You know when they said the devil is busy, well, the devil has really been busy with me since Sonya died. I've been trying to make sure I carry everything on like she would have wanted me to. Making sure our life was not disrupted a lot and the children are take care of, that they have a stable life. I got behind on some financial things and I could use the money, but you know, I'm going to pass. I'm going to put it in God's hands and let his will be done and whatever happens,

happens. If we have to make some changes, then that is what we're going to do."

"Thanks man, I really appreciate this. You know Sean, you're going to be alright. One of the reasons I know you're going to be alright is what you said about God being in control of all of our lives and destiny. Without him in our lives, it makes you wonder what the world would be like today and wonder how people who don't believe in him survive without his mercy and grace. If they only knew that he is in control and will always be in control and that when you're in his favor, there are all kinds of blessings he can bestow on you when you're going through trials and tribulations. These are just tests to see how well we handle them. Just like anything in life, if you make the wrong choice or go down the wrong road, you're going to end up at the wrong place."

CHAPTER 11

TERRELL MCDONALD

*T*errell McDonald is the next young man we're going to meet. He grew up in an adoptive parent household. Terrell's family life is not usual. His mother was a drug addict, hooked on crack. She gave Terrell up for adoption out of love actually. She knew she could not give him everything he needed and she was not strong enough to break her addiction. She ended up giving Terrell to friends of her family for adoption. One of the reasons she gave him to these friends was that they could not have children. They were not well off, but they made a decent enough living to take care of Terrell and give him whatever he needed. Terrell's mother died of an over-dose six months after giving him up for adoption. He never knew his mother, but his adoptive parents made sure he knew of her and that everything she did for him was out of love, even giving him up for adoption. And she wanted him to have a stable life where he was well taken care of and loved; that's why she gave him up. She knew that the only way he would have a chance in life was without her.

Terrell's parents were loving parents, sometimes over-compensating, because they were so glad to have a child. Terrell's adoptive mother could not have children.

Terrell was very athletically inclined. His birth mother's side of the family was well known for their athletic abilities. He had inherited a lot of their athletic traits. Anything he participated in pertaining to sports, he excelled with ease. He really excelled in football. His grades were above average, not 4.0, but good enough that it got him a football scholarship to college.

After graduation, he was drafted in the National Football League. Terrell had done really well for himself and God had played a major part in his life by giving his mother the forethought to give him up for adoption. She made sure he was placed in a home where he was loved and brought up in a Christian environment. Terrell thought about his mother often. He was always wanting to give back because God had been good to him.

He lived a normal NFL bachelor's life. Terrell came home as often as possible during his off season to visit with his parents living in the home he had purchased for them.

He also joined the staff of Pressures of a Black Man. When he came on staff, everyone could not believe how blessed they were to have someone of his statute with them. Terrell didn't have anything to gain or lose by joining the staff. He just wanted to give back because he had been so blessed by God and this was his way of giving back to the community. He wanted to make sure that he did his part and maybe someone else would be given a chance to make a change in their lives.

At Terrell's first meeting, everyone was star-struck and amazed at how down to earth he was. The young men could not believe that someone playing in the NFL was there with them. He let the staff know that he was there for them in any capacity, whether it be financial, spokesperson or just to help out. He was at their disposal. The guys were elated because they couldn't believe that they had someone of his magnitude in the organization. To give them a hand and to show that you can come from all walks of life and make it.

That is what Pressures was all about, showing the young men that they can come from all different backgrounds and still make a difference in someone else's life. The men who volunteered their time and services came from all walks of life and all kinds of backgrounds, and here's one, a superstar, to show them that they can, regardless of where you live, who you are, and where you came from, always break the cycles and make a difference.

And Terrell was really making a difference. He put Pressures of A Black Man on the map. He brought national attention and more donations. He told them what the Center was all about, to train young Black men that we have a lot of stuff just being born Black already going against us. And that they should not stack their deck with negative attitudes because the deck was already stacked against them because of their skin color. Pressures of a Black Man was trying to teach them to interact with the police in the community differently. How they should not try and infuriate them. When the police approach them in a manner that they should not, and they should make sure they do everything they can to defuse the situation. Also they should try and make sure the best possible scenario come out of all negative encounters with the police.

Terrell was the right person to speak on their behalf. Carl, Jr., and T. Max (what Terrell was called) were sitting and talking.

Carl, Jr. tells him, "Man, you know, you're doing really good, and we appreciate you coming to help us out with the guys. We do all we can, but they see us every day. Sometimes, it takes stepping out of your zone to reach these kids. It's going to take all of us, working together to make it happen. These kids are our future. What they learn today will affect how they are when they get older."

T-max said, "You know you're right. Even if we only save one, we've done something. We can only hope and pray that we make a difference in all their lives."

Carl, Jr. looked at T-max, smiled and said, "You're going to be alright and welcome abroad."

T-max said, "Thank you very much" (in his best Elvis

impersonation) and said "you know, the rapper, Lil Mike is coming to do a concert here. We should take the boys, my treat."

Carl, Jr., said, "We know. We were working on that project for the Center."

T-max said, "No problem. I'll foot the bill. It'll be nice for the boys to see him. He's from here and they will get another chance to see someone else from the community who has made it. Some of them can relate to him more than me. He can be another role model for them."

Carl, Jr. said, "I don't think that we want to use him as a role model. Even though they can relate to him and he's more on their level, I don't think he's role model material. He has done something in the past that make me not want to use him as a role model. He grew up in the foster care system. He had several charges of sexual assault against him. We could never prove anything, the girls wouldn't testify. So, we had to drop the charges. Even though we know he did it, but with the girls backing out, there was nothing we could do. That last one, if I'm not mistaken, was paid off by his record company. We couldn't prove it, so he got off again. He has a bad reputation with women, not caring about them or their feelings. What he tells one, he tells the other, not changing his game because he knows they're only there for a little while. His home environment and upbringing is the reason why he's like that with women. As for him being able to tell them that they can make a difference for themselves by following their dream, yes, but that's about it. I'll check on getting the tickets for the boys and see if he can come and speak to them while he's here. If I'm not mistaken, he's here for a whole week."

T-max said, "Okay, thanks. Just let me know what you need and come by and pick up a check. I'm going to be here so I'll be going too."

"That's good because we normally go as a group and the more help we have with the boys, the better", said Carl, Jr.

As T-max left the Center, he started thinking about all he had heard about Lil Mike's upbringing, thanking God for his mother who made sure he had a chance for a better life. Because in actuality, the foster care system could have been his reality if she had not given him up for adoption. T-max kept thinking about his life and things that had occurred and realized that God works it out all the time.

CHAPTER 12

LIL MIKE

*L*il Mike was waiting on his agent. He was furious at him for booking him a concert in his hometown. There were several days of events that his agent had booked for him.

He thought he had made it perfectly clear when he left there that he did not want anything to do with his hometown ever again. He did not want to do anything there or give anything back to it. He was fed up with it. He felt that everything bad which had happened in his life happened there and he didn't want those memories coming back. All the abuse and neglect.

Even though his agent told him there was a big chunk of money with these events, he still didn't want to do the events because of all the hurt and pain that stemmed from his hometown. Nothing positive came out of it except it gave him his drive to do better. You could hear and feel his pain in his music. Sometimes, he could not help himself. He would get so caught up in the hype and the last incident happened right before he left his hometown. One of the young ladies wanted to come back to his room and when she got there, she changed her mind. His thinking was who was she to lead him on. He ended up having his way with her and then she called the police. His agent and record company paid her off and the situation disappeared. Lil Mike didn't care what they did to make it go away, just so long as it was gone. Because if they came back to his room, they came for one thing and one thing only. By saying no didn't mean anything to him. He was a womanizer, always had been.

He never had a motherly encounter with his foster care mother. So he was just going on instinct as to how to treat women.

44

His foster parents made sure he knew it was about the money and not about them wanting to help a child in need. And they made sure he knew that there was a difference between him and their children. Lil Mike took the first opportunity he had to get out of the system and to get on his way. He had become well known for his free style abilities in rap. There was a talent contest and he entered it and won. There were representatives from his record company there and they liked what they heard and signed him and he never looked back.

His agent arrived and Lil Mike told him, "I want you to cancel the concert and find me somewhere else to go."

His agent told him, "the contract has already been signed and there is nothing we can do without being sued."

"They can sue you." Lil Mike said. "I haven't signed anything. I told you over and over again that I didn't want to go back there. They have never done nothing for me but make my life miserable."

His agent said, "the money you were getting for this contract is more than you were ever paid. So come on Mike. You're hitting them where it hurts, in their pockets. Go ahead and take their money. It's a business deal."

Lil Mike said, "Yea, but you remember what we went through the last time we were there."

"We're just going to go and do our thing, get paid, and leave without any hassle. You know something, I think you're looking to go to jail just waiting on someone to catch you in the wrong; like you got a death wish or something. If you slow down long enough, you could find the right one. Lil Mike said, "the right what? The right somebody who only want me because of the money I got, another pocket robber? They are only good for one thing and if I can't get it for free, then I pay for it. That's my no hassle policy. No, I'm not settling down; man please."

Mike's agent knew it was like talking to a stone wall. So he told Mike, "read the contract. We're going to be sued so get ready for it. I don't want you to get a reputation of breaking contracts and not showing up for concerts."

After this agent left, Mike was sitting there thinking about when he was in his hometown last. Thinking, "I'll go back and show them all. It's me, I made it and they can't do anything about it."

Mike called his agent and told him not to cancel the concert. " I'll do it."

Randy asked, "what made you change your mind." Then Randy said, "no, don't tell me. I don't want to know. I'm just glad we don't have to be sued."

Lil Mike said, "I'm going to do it but I don't want no hassle when I get there. I want to be in and out without any problems."

His agent said, "That's fine, but we are going to be there for a couple of days because it's a festival. You're the Grand Marshall in the parade, and an autograph session is at one of the local record stores. They plan on giving you the key to the city. They have planned a lot for one of their own. So, we're going to spend a couple of days and you never have to go back unless you want to."

He said, "they're going to give me, Lil Mike, their problem child of a couple of years ago, the key to their city? Now, that's what it do."

CHAPTER 13

WILLIS AND SEAN

Willis and Sean were just having small talk about how Willis knew he could make it with God on his side. Putting his faith in God and everything was going to work out for him.

Sean told him "it's okay man, you know I'm here for you if you need me."

Willis said "I really appreciated all you tried to do for me. It was talking about God that showed me that God is with us all the time. Even though you wouldn't think he would be hanging around with us and even in our darkest moments, he is with us. We just got to wait on him."

At that moment, the police did a kick door, bursting into the house. Willis and Sean were in shock. They couldn't believe what was happening. Sean remembered that there was a package in the house and only two other people besides him knew that he was going to be handling the package, Smooth and Willis.

Sean looked at Willis and said, "Man, are you wired?"

Willis said, "Man, you know I wouldn't do that to you. We go back too far for me to do that man."

Sean's attention went to Smooth. Smooth's mood was very strange the last couple of days and now he knew why. This was not like Smooth, so Sean knew they had to have threatened him to make him turn. Sean was not happy with Smooth because as he told Smooth before, this could have been handled better.

When they came in, Hardin threw Sean on the floor and said to him, "Captain, its been a long time coming, but we finally got you."

Sean looked at Hardin and said, "got me? What do you mean got me?"

Hardin asked, "isn't that package on the counter yours?"

"Package, what package?" Sean said.

"That package," Hardin said, pointing to the counter.

"I don't know anything about that package, Sean said. "I guess it was here when we got here. What's in it?"

Hardin said, "We know you had it delivered here for you. You made a mistake this time when you didn't follow your rule of thumb. No product on you or near you. Got you." Hardin said, smiling.

Captain says, "I'm not the only one in this house, so why does it have to be mine? And I'm wondering why I'm the only one in the cuffs."

Hardin told him, "don't worry, we're getting to them. We just wanted to get you first."

Sean looked at Hardin and said, "guess what, that's not my package."

Hardin stepped closer to Sean and said, "it's yours if I say its yours."

Sean looked at Hardin and said with meaning, "that s--t don't work on me Tom."

Hardin stepped back and told Sean. "I have proof that it's your package."

Sean said, "How? You got a picture of me with the package? Just because I'm in this house you assume its my package? Hell, this isn't even my house. Just a place where we get together and play cards."

Hardin says, "you're not going to weasel your way out of this one. We finally got you." Then he looks at Smith and says "book that one too. Make sure you get him. Remember the guy I told you took my starting position on the basketball team? Well,

48

that's him. What's up Willis? Never thought I would be arresting you, huh. You and your buddy, Sean. Oh, I'm sorry, Captain is what he's called here."

"You guys always thought you were better than everyone else. Now, I guess the table has turned. Didn't think you'd end up here dealing drugs with Sean."

Willis said, "I don't know what you're talking about."

Hardin said, "'they always said "birds of a feather always flock together.' You hanging out here with Captain and all proves it."

Sean looked at Hardin and then at Smith and said, "we can say the same about you two. The beat down you guys put on Smooth. What did you have to threaten him with, to make him plant that package so he could get off the hook from you? That's my defense sucker."

Hardin said, "what makes you think we beat him? He was resisting arrest and fell."

Sean said, "sure, make sure I don't fall like that. I wouldn't want anyone to get the wrong idea about you guys."

Hardin yanked him up and took him out to the patrol car. Smith brought Willis out.

Willis was thinking about his daughters. What was going to happen to them if he goes to jail for drugs.

Smith and Hardin went back in the house to help the other officers collect the other people. Nobody knew who owned the house. Everybody had keys to the house except Captain. Captain knew that whenever he wanted to go to the house, someone would always be there. He just knocked on the door and they would let him in.

Everyone was loaded up and taken down to the police station. When they got there and were booked, Sean called his lawyer and told him to come down and bail everyone out. The ones to work on first was him and his friend, Willis Hearne, because he had two daughters and he needed to get home to them.

His lawyer asked, "Sean what are they charging you with?

Sean said, "they were charging everyone with possession. The police kicked the door down at the house and because there was drugs in the house, they arrested everyone. No one was in possession of the drugs at the time and no one claimed the package as theirs. But here, the trip about everything with all the people in the house, they wanted to put the drugs on me, saying they're mine. You know they have been trying to get me on the charge for a long time, and the one time I just happened to be in a place where there are some drugs, they're trying to get me through Smooth by threatening him. You know Smooth, he would never do this unless he was being threaten by them. I can't blame him. I might have done the same thing in his shoes. They can't prove anything just because I was in a house where there were drugs. The house is not mine. I don't even have a key. It's just a place to hang out and play cards."

His lawyer asked, "what's the deal with your friend, Willis."

Sean said, "he's innocent. He just happened to be at the wrong place at the wrong time. That's all to that. He is a family man, just lost his wife to breast cancer, and raising two daughters alone."

The lawyer asked, "why was he there."

Sean told him, "We were just talking, reminiscing; he and I have known each other since high school. We played on the same basketball team together. We were the Michael Jordan-Scottie Pippin on the team. We were catching up on old times when the cops kicked the door down. It's like I said, he was just at the wrong place at the wrong time."

50

The lawyer said, "I will do the best I can to rush this"

Sean said, "sure, with all the money I'm paying you guys, I better be out of here pretty quick."

CHAPTER 14

WILLIS AND SEAN COMMUNITY SERVICE

Willis and Sean were sitting in the cell and Willis looked at Sean and said, "What did they mean when they said they can't believe they got you because you don't have drugs around you?"

Sean told Willis, "this was the first time I have ever had drugs in my presence. I have never handled anything personally. I did this for you because of your family situation. I didn't want you out there doing something stupid. So I decided to do this for you myself."

"Well, if no one knew but me and you," Willis said, "I didn't tell anyone and I know you didn't turn yourself in. What happened?"

Sean said, "There was a third party but they didn't know what I wanted the package for or about you. They knew it was an unusual request for me. Everything is going to be okay and that person will be dealt with in time once we get out."

When Sean went back to the house after the lawyer bailed everybody out, he asked if anyone had seen Smooth. No one had seen him for awhile. Sean said that's fine.

Later on, Sean got a phone call from his lawyer telling him that this is just the first offense for him and his friend, Willis. But because they can't prove whose drugs they were, they have to charge everyone there.

The lawyer said, "the judge assigned you guys to a Center called Pressures of a Black Man for community service. They want you bad enough even though they know they can't do anything to you but hold you on possession. That's

52

why they recommended community service. The community service to them with the Center will be more of a punishment to you because of what they stand for. The program is set up like a big brother program for Blacks, to be a mentor for them. This community service, if you ask me, was given as a joke. Like saying who would want you as a role model with your history. With all the focus in the community these days against police brutality and drugs, you and your buddy need to go to this Center and register."

While Sean was registering at the Center, Willis came in.

He walked over to him and said, "Thank you man. I appreciate you because I don't know what I would have done if you hadn't gotten me out. I was really strung out and not thinking about how I needed to go about things at home. But this showed me that God is always with me because we could be doing jail time. I'm telling you man, he's with me and I don't know why I ever doubted him. If there's anything I can ever do for you, let me know."

Sean said, "its all good."

Carl, Jr. got a report that the Judge had assigned him two new volunteers. He looked at the names and wondered where he knew them. Then he realized who they were, Sean Moore and Willis Hearne - the Michael Jordan and Scottie Pippen of their time. As he read the report, he found out that Sean Moore is Captain, a very powerful drug dealer. He thought what kind of joke are they playing. Carl, Jr. sat there thinking to himself about God trying to tell him something. Maybe it's his way of making a change in Sean/Captain's life.

After the initial orientation in the program, they let Sean and Willis know that they planned on taking of boys to the Lil Mike concert. The volunteers are serving as Chaperons for the group. They both told Carl, Jr. that they would be there.

CHAPTER 15

LIL MIKE ARRIVES IN HIS HOMETOWN

*L*il Mike and his crew checked into the hotel. His Road Manager had taken care of everything except now he wanted a car so he could go visit the old neighborhood.

Randy, his agent, was getting worried now and said, "I thought you didn't want to do any sight-seeing, just do the functions we're being paid for and leave."

"Excuse me," Lil Mike said, "but I think you work for me and what's the problem? I really don't appreciate you questioning me on what I'm doing. I'm going to take a shower and when I get out of the shower and get dressed, have my car out front. What the hell. This might be what I need while I'm here."

Lil Mike's agent was not stunned by the language he used. He could go off at a drop of a dime. He just hoped this was not going to bring back the old problems they had with him: the drugs, the women, and the drinking.

He was back in his hometown. He had been on the straight and narrow since the last jam that they got him out of. But he was on familiar grounds and some of the same people were still here. For one thing, Randy noticed that he was overly friendly with the desk clerk. She didn't realize that he does that all the time every where he goes. Randy knew he considered her a groupie, just like all the rest of them. He was not interested in her for a serious relationship, just a good time while he was there. He had a way with women, making them think he was the answer to all their problems. And he was, but the twist is only while he was there; then it was on to the next.

Randy just hoped he could keep a close watch on him and

54

leave this city with as few problems as possible. Now he knew what it meant when people said "money isn't everything" and he felt like this saying really was going to be put to the test while they were here. He called and made sure Lil Mike's car was ready.

Mike, on his way out, stopped by the desk and whispered something to Amber. Randy was watching him and he turned around and winked at her, smiling and walking out of the hotel. Randy thought, "here we go again."

Lil Mike was driving around and just looking at the neighborhood. He went past one of the foster homes and the memories of all the pain and abuse came back. He speeded off peeling rubber. Upon speeding away, he didn't notice that there was a police car parked. They hit their siren and pulled him over. When the cops got out of the patrol car, guess who they were? Hardin and Smith.

Officer Smith asked "driver's license, registration and proof of insurance."

Lil Mike said, "the car is rented as stated on the tags, commercial," very sarcastically.

Smith said, "there is no reason for the sarcasm."

Lil Mike said, "man, why all the hassle?"

Smith said, "no hassle, just got you doing 65 in a 35."

Mike said, "you know what, you're probably right. Just give my ticket so I can go. As a matter of act, I know I was speeding, just give me my ticket so I can go. I confess."

At that moment, Hardin walked up. He had been running the tag on the car. "So, looks like life been treating you good. But I can't believe you had the nerve to show back up here. Just because you got money don't mean you got the right to come back here and drive like a bat out of hell."

Lil Mike turned around and asked Hardin, "what the f--k

he was talking about. Who the hell are you?"

Hardin said, "nigger, who the f--k you think you are talking to?"

Lil Mike said, "I know your a-s didn't call me a 'nigger'."

Hardin told Mike, "turn around and put your hands on the car."

"What," Mike said, "you're going to arrest me after calling me a nigger? Man, your a-s is crazy, always f--king with people."

Harding pulled his night stick out of his belt and went to hit Lil Mike with it.

Smith stopped him saying, "we got enough problems already. We can't afford to have them investigating us more. Let's handle this the right way. He's guilty of speeding. We got him for resisting arrest."

Hardin said, "yea, you're right" and threw him up against the car and put the cuffs on too tight.

Lil Mike said, "Man you know these cuffs are too tight. Can you loosen them up some?"

Hardin looked at Mike and said "you talking to me? Oh, I don't think you're talking to me," as he bumped his head as he put him in the car.

Lil Mike was furious because he didn't deserve to be treated like this because he was Lil Mike, a star coming home to do something for his community and to be treated like this.

After they got to the station, they let him make his phone call. He called Randy to come and get him out of jail. He told Randy that he had been arrested for speeding and resisting arrest.

Randy said, "okay, I'm on my way, do you have your medicine with you."

Lil Mike said, "yea, man, come get me."

Randy couldn't believe this. They had only been in town for one and it had already started.

Lil Mike said, "hurry up, they're crazy. I don't know what they're going to do to me in here."

Randy said, "it's going to take our lawyers a long time to get here, but there is a group who is coming to the concert, and they had a lawyer to call for you to speak to them at the Center. I'll get him to help. His name is Steven Young."

Randy called Steven and told him what he knew and Steven told Randy that he would meet him at the station. Randy was pacing the floor when Steven walked in.

Steven walked over and introduced himself - "Steven Young"

"Randy Jones, Mike's agent."

Steven told Randy, "I have to make a couple of phone calls, and let me see what I can do. This should take less than thirty minutes."

Randy said, "okay" and started back pacing the floor.

The doors opened and Lil Mike walked out, looking angry and furious, yelling "you see why I didn't want to come back here. These m--rf--kers are crazy. Every time you look around, they're doing some dumb s--t."

Randy told Lil Mike, "calm down and let's get out of here."

But this time, Lil Mike had gotten out of control, saying stuff like "these m--rf--kers ain't good enough to tie my shoes, f--k them all." Mike was going out the door, just as Hardin and Smith were coming through it. Hardin has this big smirk on his face, walked by Lil Mike coming face-to-face with him looking eyeball-to-eyeball.

Hardin said in a low voice as he passes Mike, "you got lucky nigger."

Mike grabbed Hardin and said "man I will fuck you up."

57

Smith jumped in between them.

Hardin said, "its okay, I made a mistake and stepped on his foot. Sorry man, didn't mean to."

Randy told Lil Mike, "let it go, you have too much going for you man. Please Mike, don't let him get to you like this."

Lil Mike said, "yea man, I'll show him.

"Show me, show me what?" Hardin said. "You better make it good and pray to God as he goes out the door."

Randy was still trying to calm Lil Mike down in the car.

Lil Mike was saying stuff like "I can't believe how they think they can treat you like s--t and get away with it. Every time you look around, they are man-handling somebody. There is all kinds of s--t going on with this police department. I might have been wrong, but they're more wrong than me. Why do we have to always get the short end of the stick, all the time? We always have to deal with some redneck cop f-----g with us. I guess we're on the wrong side of the color line. Man, let's just get this s--t over with so we can leave and never look back."

As they are walking through the lobby of the hotel, Lil Mike looks over at the lobby desk, looking for Amber and she was looking at him like he was her savior; he was going to get her out of this town. She didn't realize that he is not her savior; he is not anyone's savior.

CHAPTER 16

AMBER GETS HER CHANCE WITH MIKE

*M*ike went to his room and laid across the bed thinking about all kinds of things he wanted to do to f--k the cop up.

Randy's voice started to break through his thoughts, telling him to "snap out of it. Don't slip back, think positive. Don't look back and be dragged down by this. I talked to Steven Young about the cop and he said that they are investigating them as we speak."

Lil Mike said, "alright man, I'm going to let you handle this, but if I see them again, I don't know how I'm going to handle it. I wasn't strapped this time, but if I go out from now on, you can bet I'll be carrying a piece. I'm not going to be treated like that again. I know my rights. I can say what I want just as long as I cooperate with them. They think they can say anything to us and when we respond back, we're in the wrong."

Randy told him again, "man, let us take care of this legally. You got too much going for you to let this stop you. All we have to do is pay the ticket. Steven can get the resisting arrest charge thrown out because of everything going on with those two. Just hang in there; let's not fall back to where we first started, we've come too far to do that now."

"Okay Randy," Mike said, "I'm going to trust you. But you know how much I trust you, don't you?"

Randy said, "yea, as far as you can throw me. No problem man, I'll take that," and he walked out the door.

Lil Mike, laid back on the bed. The phone rang and it was Amber, saying she was calling to check on him because when he walked through the lobby, he didn't say anything.

"I just wanted to know if you were okay and if there was anything I could do," she said.

Mike said,"no, I'm alright, just been a long day and a few problems. Nothing I can't handle. What time you get off?"

She said, "in an hour."

Why don't you come up after your shift," Mike said.

Amber said "okay."

Lil Mike was thinking "here's this white girl who would do anything to be with me. I know one thing, she thinks that I may be her ticket out of this town. Her "knight in shining armor." He would be her knight alright, just for the next couple days anyway. He laid back and took a nap, waking up when Amber knocked on the door.

Lil Mike made it a night to remember for her. He was everything she thought he would be. If only she knew, that was him with all the groupies. She was in love, he was the one. She left the next morning smiling. Lil Mike had rolled over and asked if he would see her tonight. She said if he wanted to. He said yes. Why change to a new groupie when you have just a couple more days. He told her to be prepared to stay the night. She said okay. He rolled back over and fell asleep.

Randy couldn't sleep for thinking about how he was going to make sure Lil Mike stayed out of trouble the next couple of days. He went down to the weight room to relieve some stress. After working out for an hour, waiting for the elevator, he realized how tired he was. The door to the elevator opened and out walked Amber, looking embarrassed that he had seen her. Randy realized that he had to be on his game to ensure that she not get hurt and Lil Mike stayed out of trouble.

Amber went to work the next day on top of the world. She didn't tell anyone that she had spent the night with Lil Mike.

Everyone was talking about the concert and she felt like she had the inside scoop because she slept with Lil Mike. If only she had known that he was like this with all the women he met on tour. She was just a body while he was there and when he left, she would never hear from him again. She was assuming that because he was so personal and intimate with her, she meant something to him.

That night, Amber went back to his room. They watched movies and he massaged her feet. This made Amber feel like she was in heaven and things couldn't be more perfect. She didn't spend the next night because he had a function to go to. Amber was at the front desk and she heard some of her co-workers talking about another co-worker who said she had a date with Lil Mike after his visit to the Center. She was devastated with what she heard and couldn't believe he would do this to her after all they shared.

CHAPTER 17

LIL MIKE AT THE CENTER

S teven called Randy and told him that everything was set up for tonight and he would see them at 7:00.

Lil Mike went to the Center and gave them a good speech. He told them that the only person stopping them from accomplishing anything is themselves. Nothing in the world is unattainable. They are the only ones who can put limits on themselves. They should set goals and make them happen. Whatever they wanted to accomplish, find out what it takes to make it happen, and then make it happen. He said, "You have to make your dream come true. If you can't sell yourself, no one else can sell you either."

Everyone was amazed at how much he had matured since the last time he was in town. Lil Mike signed autographs and talked to the boys. There was one boy Mike took a liking to, Tristen, because he was in the same situation he had been in. Tristen was coming up through the foster care system just like Lil Mike. Mike and Tristen talked about their story not really going into all the details but enough so that they both knew what the other one was going through and had gone through. Lil Mike told Tristen to keep his head up. He had to go through some of the same problems. Life is not fair sometimes, but we have to make the best of what we got until we can do better.

"When you don't know any better, you can't do better, but when you know better, you do better," Mike said.

Tristen gave Mike a hug, "thank you for listening to me. No one ever takes time out to care about what I have to say. The only time I ever felt like someone cared about what happened to

62

me is when I am at the Center. The Center is great for all of us. It takes our minds off our problems while we are here. We do a lot of activities together. We even have a rap group - we're pretty good too."

Mike laughed and asked them if they wanted to perform for him. Maybe they could be one of his opening acts if they were any good.

Randy was really surprised at Lil Mike's interest in the young men at the Center. Both Mike and Randy were surprised at the group's performance. They had something. Randy and Mike told them that they were going to open for him. Everyone was cheering and full of excitement. They couldn't believe their luck.

Mike getting ready to leave, turned and said to them,"I enjoyed my visit and I will see you tomorrow at the concert." He looked at Tristen and told him that he would see him back stage. Tristen smiled and said, "okay, bye."

Steven and Carl, Jr. walked Randy and Lil Mike out. Lil Mike told Carl, Jr. that Tristen's group had something and he wanted to help them. "I never wanted to help anyone, always believing since no one helped me, why bother or try to give anything back."

Steven told Lil Mike, "Tristen doesn't talk a lot; he's just involved with his music. He is really dedicated to his music. We all thought he was talented, but what do we know."

Steven and Carl, Jr. told them goodbye.

Steven told Carl, Jr., "this could be the best thing to ever happen to Tristen and the Center. Maybe this will change Lil Mike's attitude about a whole lot of things. I know after the concert everything around here is going to change. We're going to have some egos to deal with. I hope Lil Mike is on the up and up with Tristen and his group. These kids don't need any more disappointments.

CHAPTER 18

LIL MIKE'S ENCOUNTER WITH AMBER

R andy and Lil Mike went back to the hotel.

Mike told Randy, "I made a date with one of the girls in the hotel, but I don't want to be bothered."

Randy said, "the desk clerk?"

Mike told him, "no. I decided to change up. A whole lot of things have happened in these last couple of days. Getting arrested, going to the Center, I just need to do a lot of thinking about what's next for me. I really want to do something for Tristen and his group."

Randy told Lil Mike, "that's no problem because in your contract, you can develop new talent. They can be your first group."

Lil Mike, smiling, said "that'll work, and don't forget to get rid of the girl and I will see you in the morning."

Randy told Mike, "I'm glad that you're trying to get your head on straight."

Mike said, "it's time I made a change. There's just so much I want to say and the only way I can express myself at this moment is through my music. I'm going to try and look at life differently from now on."

Randy said, "that's great. You got a lot of talent, but the way you are going right now, I don't think you can make it without changing."

Mike told Randy, "You're probably right and hey, what the hell, I can't do worst than I'm doing right now."

Closing the door behind him, Mike decides to take a shower and lay down. He felt a change, but he couldn't put his finger on it. Something happened to make him feel this way. Maybe it was going to the Center and meeting Tristen and the other guys. He felt this was the first good night's sleep he was going to get in a long time.

Randy went and found the young lady and told her Mike had changed his mind about tonight. Amber overheard Randy and figured this was her time to find out if she meant anything to him. She went up to Mike's room later on that night and knocked on the door several times before he opened it, looking sleepy.

He asked her, "what's up?"

She asked, "can I come in?"

He told her, "I'm not in the mood for company."

She insisted on coming in. He let her come in, thinking the quicker he let her get whatever was on her mind off, the quicker he could get back to sleep.

She says, "I think I've fallen in love with you."

Mike said, "love, you don't even know me. You have no idea who I am, just what you've heard."

She said, "because of the way you treated me and acted around me."

She said, "there's no way you can treat someone like that and not have feelings for them."

Mike said, "really, I didn't think you had to have feelings for someone to have sex. Yes, sex, that's all it was for me."

Amber said, " you're wrong. We were not just having sex. Those last two nights we spent together were wonderful."

He told her, "I have women in every city I go to. If not one, then two or however many I want. All we had was sex and if you made more out of it, then that's your problem, not mine."

Amber walked over to Mike and tried to kiss him. He pushed her away and tells her, "you have to leave."

She is furious and says, "I'm not leaving."

65

He told her, "you can leave on your own or I will have you put out."

Amber started screaming, "you can't treat people like this and think you can get away with it. I'm not leaving."

Mike said, "I told you when I opened the door that I didn't want any company, but no, you insisted on coming in, and now, because I'm not behaving like you think I should, I'm the bad guy. I never promised you or anybody else anything. We had a good time, that's all. Now, I want you to leave."

She said, " fine, I'm going."

Amber left and Lil Mike went back to sleep.

CHAPTER 19

LIL MIKE'S LAST ENCOUNTER WITH THE POLICE

A couple of hours later, there was another knock on the door. Lil Mike, furious now, thinking it was Amber back at the door opened it and yelled "what the hell's wrong with you?"

Amber not standing there, but Hardin and Smith were.

Mike said, "I guess all the harassment in the street wasn't enough. You got to come to my room to finish it. What you want now?"

Hardin pushed Mike back, turning him around and throwing him on the floor, putting his knee in his back in the process.

He tells Lil Mike, "you are under arrest for rape."

Mike tried to turn and look at Hardin. "Rape! Raped who?"

"You're under arrest for the rape of the desk clerk downstairs. She is on her way to the hospital as we speak. She has been badly beaten too," Hardin said.

Lil Mike said, "I didn't rape her, let alone beat her. I don't have to rape nobody to have sex. Do you know who I am?"

Hardin said, "I don't give a dam who you are. You're under arrest" and he read him his rights, then started to take him downstairs.

Mike yelled for Randy, whose room is next door.

Randy heard the noise and ran to Lil Mike's room and asked, "what's going on."

Smith turned and said to him, "we are arresting Lil Mike

for the rape of Amber Chase."

Randy asked, "who's Amber Chase."

Smith said, "the desk clerk and she is on her way to the hospital as we speak. She said Mike raped her tonight."

Randy looked at Lil Mike as Lil Mike is yelling, "man, I didn't do it. If you ever believed me, believe me now. I didn't do it. She came by wanting to stay, but I told her I didn't want any company. She got mad and stormed out. She had to have been beaten up by someone else because I sure as hell didn't do it. That b---h is lying if she said I did it. She is trying to get back at me."

Hardin said, "oh yea, you're innocent alright. Just like you were innocent the last time you were arrested for rape and your record company paid your way out of that one."

Lil Mike said, "F--k you man, I didn't do anything to that b---h. Yea, we had sex, but it was consensual by both of us. And tonight, she came by my room wanting to spend the night. I told her I didn't want company. She didn't want to leave. So I threatened her with having her thrown out. I didn't touch her, but no matter what I say, you're going to think I did. Take me and book me for rape; when its all over, we will see who has the last laugh. You know why I'm going to have the last laugh? DNA, you heard of that? Wait until the DNA test comes back, then we'll see who'll be laughing then. And if she does have my DNA, its going to show it's not recent. Ever watch CSI lately? Modern technology, a m----rf-----r."

Hardin said, "you're telling us you're going to give us your DNA?"

Mike said, "Hell, yea, I haven't got anything to hide."

Randy told Mike, "don't do anything stupid. Let them get a warrant if they want it. I'm calling Steven Young and tell him to meet us at the police station."

Hardin pulled Lil Mike off the bed and acted like he accidentally elbowed Mike in the mouth. Lil Mike, tasting blood, spit it out on the bed.

Hardin tells Smith, "collect the bed linen because that was evidence (DNA)."

Mike said, "You're going to owe me the biggest apology you ever had to give. You better hope I don't sue you. You guys are acting like renegade cops. We will always have a hard time, nothing is going to change as long as we have cops like you on the police force, going around harassing people, thinking every Black man has something to hide or has done something wrong. Just because we want to make a better life for ourselves; drive a nice car, dress a little different, play our music a little louder. You are in for a rude awakening because I did not rape that girl or beat her up. She is just trying to get back at me."

Hardin said, "So you're telling me someone else beat her and raped her."

"I'm not telling you anything," Mike said. "All I know is I didn't do it. Now what happened to her, your guess is as good as mine."

Randy told Mike, " don't say another word. Wait until they meet with Steven Young to figure out what's really going on."

Mike said, "as soon as I can leave, I'm leaving. We are not doing the concert, they can sue me for all I care. I knew it was a mistake to come here in the first place. Never again."

Randy told Mike, "stay calm, we are going to get you out."

Mike said, " I want to spend as little time as possible in jail."

Randy called Steven and explained what he knew. Steven agreed to meet them. While getting dressed, he called Carl,

Jr. and told him that there was a situation going on with Lil Mike and to meet him at the police station. Steven told Carl, Jr., their two favorite cops were involved. Carl, Jr. said he was on his way.

Carl, Jr. was on his way to the station when he noticed a patrol car parked on the side of the road. And he was trying to figure out what the officers were doing. As he got closer, he saw there was a person on the ground. He then realized that it was Hardin and Smith. They looked surprised when he ran over like they had been caught doing something wrong.

He asked, "Why do you guys have him out here? He is suppose to be on his way to the police station."

Hardin said, "he claimed he was having a seizure and started jerking in the back of the car. So we took him out so he wouldn't hurt himself. And when we got him out, he was still jerking. And that is when you drove up."

Smith said, "he's dead."

Hardin said, "we didn't do anything to him."

Carl, Jr. said. "Yea, right. Just like you didn't beat up Smooth. I guess he was resisting arrest too."

Hardin grabbed Carl, Jr. by the collar and said, "I don't have to answer to you. Who do you think you are? It's just like we said, he was resisting arrest. If you start trouble, you'll be surprised at what I can do and what I know. You can go to help a fellow officer one day and end up like your father. Just like your father went to help, you could be in the same situation and get the same results."

Carl, Jr. yanked away from Hardin and said to him, "if you ever put your hands on me or threaten me again, you won't live to see another day."

Hardin tells him, "you don't scare me."

Carl, Jr. tells them, "this is the straw that broke the camel's

70

back. There is no way you guys can talk your way out of this one."

Hardin walked up to Carl, Jr., nose to nose, and said, "if you ever hint that we did something to Lil Mike, you might as well live with your family every hour of the day because you can't be in two places at the same time. And you will drop your guard."

Carl, Jr. looked at Hardin and said, "if you touch my wife or son, I'll kill you, how about that?"

Carl, Jr. looked at the situation he was in with only himself alone with Smith and Hardin and knew what kind of danger he was in. He went back to his car and checked on the back up.

Hardin told the officers the same story he told Carl, Jr. and Smith confirmed it.

CHAPTER 20

CARL, JR. TALKS TO CYNTHIA

C arl, Jr. went home and was very disturbed by all that had been going on. Especially when Hardin mentioned his father like he knew something wasn't right with the way he died. He was going to find out what happened to Lil Mike and why he died. He knew in his heart that Hardin and Smith had something to do with how he died. These were the same cops in the middle of all the problems with the department. The same two. If they were not held accountable for this, there was no telling how the city was going to react to Lil Mike's death. His death was the last straw the community could take. He knew that this would be a way the Black community would validate all their claims of abuse.

When he went home, Cynthia was waiting up for him. She knew when he ran out that he would need her when he got home.

He told her, "baby, this city is in for a lot of trouble. We're sitting on a time bomb that could blow-up at any time. He told her he thought Hardin and Smith had killed Lil Mike and about how Hardin had implied that something was not right with his father's death. Most of all, he threatened you and Lil Carl. That's when I knew he has to be stopped."

Carl, Jr. tells his wife, "you will have to be careful because Hardin was like a mad man, now that his back was up against the wall. There's no telling what he'll do now that he thinks I'm on to him. When IA starts their investigation into this case, there's no telling what he's going to do."

She told him, "I will be careful, but I am not going to let

72

him take control of our lives. God is always watching over us and you know that. Even if we slip, God doesn't, and if Hardin happens to do something, then it will only be God's will. There's no other way to look at it. If I were to look at it differently, I know I would be scared to death of Hardin. He would be in control, but I know God is in control. So we're going to let his will be done. We're going to put it in God's hands and let it go. There's nothing going to happen to us unless it's God's will. Even if our lives are taken, we have to know God doesn't make mistakes."

Carl, Jr. said, "that's why I love you. You always know what to say."

She said, "this is true, now go to sleep."

Carl, Jr. woke up and turned on the television news and as he expected, the city was in turmoil. Everybody wanted answers about how could this have happened. How did this young man on his way to the police station end up dead before he got there. And the only witnesses to his death are the two officers who are being investigated for police brutality. They're both telling the same story - that he had a seizure and before they could get him to the hospital, he died. There's another witness who came up after the fact, but guess what, he's another police officer. They were saying when will we as citizens know the truth.

CHAPTER 21

AMBER'S GUILT

A mber was sitting in the hospital emergency prep-room and she heard a lot of commotion. She heard the nurses talking about a DOA coming and the DOA was the rapper who came into town for the festival. She thought she was dreaming. This can not be happening. He can't be dead.

She kept saying, "he can't be dead," over and over real low at first, but getting louder and louder. She went into hysterics and they tried to calm her down. They assumed her hysteria was over being raped, not realizing that she knew she was the reason why Lil Mike was dead. Not actually killing him, but if she hadn't accused him of rape, he would probably be alive.

Amber passed out after the doctor gave her something to calm her down. When she woke up, her world started closing back in on her. She realized what she had to do now. She rang the bell for the nurse and asked her to get a police officer to her room.

The police officer asked, "are you ready to give your statement about your rape."

Amber said, "no, a murder."

The policeman looked confused and said, "But I was told to take your statement on being raped. Am I in the wrong room?"

She said, "no, I'm talking about Lil Mike's murder."

He told her, "hold on I'll call for the Police Captain."

When the Captain got there, Amber told him, "I am the reason why Lil Mike is dead, because he never raped me. I wanted to get back at him for the way he treated me. All these bruises

I did them myself to be convincing."

The Police Captain arrested her saying, "you falsified a police report and I don't know what other charges that could be filed because of this situation. As soon as you are able to be released, you will be taken into custody."

Amber lay back in her bed and started saying over and over, "I didn't mean it." She went into total hysterics again, uncontrollable. The doctor now knows the whole story of why she was so hysterical now and before. Her guilt had sent her over the edge. They had to admit her to the psychiatric ward.

CHAPTER 22

THE BEGINNING OF THE END

*J*ohn Smith is sitting in his house. Just him and his dog, because he is not married. His dog is the only family he has. He is writing a letter to Officer Jackson. He had learned that Lil Mike was telling the truth about not raping Amber Chase. Everything he said was the truth and now he's dead. All because he wouldn't take a stand against Hardin. Even though he did not kill Lil Mike directly, he felt responsible because he let Hardin get his way. He had asked for another partner, but too late. He was writing this letter to let everyone know what really happened that night when Lil Mike died.

Smith was hoping to find Carl, Jr. at the Center, but Carl, Jr. had not made it in yet. There was a young man standing outside the Center and he asked if he would give the letter to Officer Carl Jackson, Jr.

Smith said, "tell him I'm sorry and this letter will explain everything that he wanted to know."

Carl, Jr., before leaving home that day, reminded his wife, Cynthia to "be careful while you're out because with it coming out that Lil Mike was not guilty of rape, there is no telling what that nut case Hardin is up to."

She told him, "I prayed on it and I'm through with it. I don't know why you're worried because you know the Lord is on our side and Hardin doesn't stand a chance."

Cynthia was fixing breakfast that morning and realized how much she really loved this man and how much he meant to her. She prayed that God would keep him safe and strong in his faith.

76

Carl, Jr. headed for work and told Cynthia "don't forget to pick up Lil Carl from football practice."

She yelled at him as he was going out the door,"I haven't, I love you."

CHAPTER 23

HARDIN'S PLAN

*H*ardin had devised a plan to make sure Jackson kept his mouth closed even though he didn't really know anything. He was just trying to make things hard. He also knew he didn't need any extra trouble because of all the other investigations. This one could be the one that did it for him and he knew it.

Hardin called and left a message with the Receptionist that Carl, Jr.'s son had been in an accident at football practice, and he needed to come and pick him up.

When Carl, Jr. got to the Center, he was told that someone had called and said that he needed to pick up his son from football practice because he had been in an accident. Carl, Jr. turned and ran out of the Center. He knew in his heart that Hardin had something to do with it. There was no doubt in his mind. He kept trying to reach Cynthia on her cell phone, but she didn't answer and he didn't understand why because he knows she would keep it on because of what was going on with Hardin.

When he reached the playing field, Lil Carl was practicing right along side the other players. He called Lil Carl over and told him his mother will pick him up. Lil Carl told his father that he was spending the night with his friend, Tim, because his mother wanted to surprise him with dinner. Then Carl, Jr., realizes the target was not Lil Carl, but Cynthia. He turned and ran to his car trying to reach her on her cell phone to make sure she was all right.

The reason he couldn't reach her on the phone was because she was inside one of the local stores, picking up somethings that she needed for dinner and her phone had dropped out of her purse when she got out of her car.

When she came out of the store and got into her car and pulled out of the parking lot, she didn't realize that someone had been watching and waiting on her. She started looking for her cell phone to call Carl, Jr. and tell him not to be late for dinner because she planned a special evening for them.

When she looked in her rear view mirror, she saw police lights but no siren. Cynthia fumbled through her purse for her phone because she knew this was not good. When the patrol car hit the siren for her to pull over, she really got nervous and started praying to God, no.

When the cop stared to walk to her car, looking in her side mirror, she saw it was Hardin from all the publicity. She knew she was in trouble because she didn't know what he had planned.

He asked her, "exit the vehicle."

She gets out of the car and asked, "what's the problem."

He said, "no problem. I've just got a call that someone fitting your description had just shoplifted the store you just left."

She said, "shoplift? You know I wouldn't shoplift. You know who I am, you're just playing a game with me."

He tells her. "I need to search your car. I'm just doing my job."

Cynthia asked, "why would I steal knowing my husband is a police officer and disgrace him."

He said, "Are you saying that being a wife of a police officer gives you a get out of jail pass. Put your hands on the vehicle and spread your legs."

He started acting like he was searching her but was actually groping and being too familiar and up close, and intimidating with his searching of her. She could not believe what he was doing in his search of her. She was in total disgust over his behavior. Just as he finished, he whispered in her ear and said, "tell your husband I said hello and you to have a nice day. They must have been mistaken in the description."

He walked back to his car whistling. She could not believe what had just happened, standing there with her hands still on her car. She then realized how desperate he was. She got in her car feeling like she had been raped. She was crying as she drove off, thinking how far will this go and what if he hurt Lil Carl. She jumped out of her car, when she got home, leaving everything in the car and the door opened. She entered the house not closing the door completely, running up stairs pulling her clothes off as she ran leaving a trail of them. All she wanted to do was shower to get the stench of his hands off her body.

When Carl, Jr. got home, he saw her car door opened. He ran into the house and saw the trail of her clothes. He started calling out her name, "Cynthia, Cynthia, where are you baby," picking up her clothes as he went up the stairs.

He looked up and saw her coming down the stairs while picking up her clothes. He pulled her in his arms and asked her "what did he do. Did he rape you?"

She pulled him away and said, "no, but you better fix this problem fast." She then tells him the story through tears. He looked at her and realized that this is a turning point in his life. This man has just violated his family and threatened him to keep him silent about what he thought happened to Lil Mike. He knew it was time for him to give up his badge.

CHAPTER 24

JOHN SMITH'S LETTER

C arl, Jr. went back to the Center to talk to Steven about his decision. When he walked in, the Receptionist said, "I forgot to give you this. Tristen said a White man left this letter for you. He said it looked like one of the cops who was involved with Lil Mike's death."

Carl, Jr. grabbed the letter and tore it open. As he started to read it, he started laughing and yelling, "we got him, we got him." Steven heard all the commotion and came out of his office.

He asked Carl, Jr., "what's going on."

Carl, Jr. grabbed Steven and told him, "we got that son of a b---h Hardin. Read this."

Steven said, "I think you're right, but we need to find Smith first because by the sound of this, he's planning to eat his gun."

Carl, Jr. called the Police Captain to find out where Hardin and Smith were. His Captain told him that Hardin was with IA and Smith never showed up.

"Captain," he said, "I got some information concerning the case, but first, can you get me Smith's address. I think he's going to do something to hurt himself." The Captain got the address.

Carl, Jr. told the Captain, " thanks and I'll give you a full report in person. I'm on my way there."

The Captain said, " okay."

Carl, Jr. then gave Steven the address to Smith's house, which was not too far from the Center. He asked Steven, "find him and bring him to the station, if it's not too late."

Steven said, "okay, I'm on it man" and he left.

Carl, Jr. was on his way out of the Center when he received a call that an Officer was in need of assistance and it gave Smith's address. He began praying that they get there in time.

Carl, Jr. started reading the rest of Smith's letter. Smith told of how he always wanted to be a police officer, but fate wasn't on his side because having been placed with Hardin, his career was over. He realized that because he did nothing to stop Hardin, he was as much to blame because he not only didn't do anything to stop him but also did not report it either. He wrote that he didn't want to make any waves but chose the blue shield of silence instead. He wanted to clear his slate.

He wrote that Hardin had done all the things he had ever been accused of and that he knew the whole story behind Carl Jackson, Sr.'s death. Harding knew that Carl, Sr. was shot by the officer who he came to help instead of the assailant as they originally stated in the official report they gave. Carl, Sr. had walked up on a pay-off that had gone bad. The drug dealer was tired of being hassled by the officer. Then he pulled a gun and they were struggling and the officer had seduced him when Carl, Sr. walked up. The drug dealer started to explain to Carl, Sr. thinking he was in on the extortion that he was tired of the payoffs. He stated the pay-off kept going up higher and higher until he wouldn't be able to pay. The officer knew the drug dealer had just sealed Carl, Sr.'s faith. The officer shot the drug dealer and asked Carl, Sr. for his gun, then shot him with his gun without even blinking an eye and that was the real story.

The letter also contained details on all the things that he and Hardin had done which he thought were questionable, including setting up Smooth to turn on Captain so they could make a big collar. Smith was bearing his soul. He could not live with

82

himself any more. The fact that Lil Mike died had an effect on him since he could have changed the situation, but here again, did nothing and now it came back to haunt him. Because Lil Mike had been wrongly accused, he could not believe that he let Hardin lead him down the wrong path because he didn't want to stand out or make waves. His faith in God had been shaken to the core. He knew how far he had sunk into despair and how Hardin and all his negativity had rubbed off on him. Even though he thought that when he went home, because he didn't participate, he could hold on to his humanity. Even though he didn't condone what Hardin did, he didn't do anything to stop him either, so it was just as bad.

Smith's letter also said that Hardin more than likely would go after his wife and son. He had no remorse for anything he had done. He justified everything he did by holding on to how much he despised Blacks. He felt that if Willis hadn't taken his starting position on the basketball team, he wouldn't be stuck in a job he hated. Hardin had become more infuriated since they had arrested Willis Hearne, the guy who he claims ruined his life and because he didn't do anything with the opportunity he had of going professional. Talking of when Willis got his girlfriend pregnant and married her and did nothing with the opportunity. Hardin was like a time bomb he wrote. Hardin always thought that with him being White, he didn't have to put forth any extra effort. He felt his behavior was justified because it was just the way he was brought up. He believed affirmative action was something that Blacks cooked up to keep the White man down.

Smith also said in the letter that there was a couple of things that could happen with him. He would see him at the police station or he could be at his funeral. He prayed to God that he take it out his heart the desire to kill himself. He wrote that he didn't think he could deal with the fallout from all that had happened. It's going to be drastic; there was no way around it.

Officer Hardin was being questioned by IA about the Michael Edward's case, aka Lil Mike. They told him that at this moment, they can't find any discrepancies and he could go. If they needed him after they talked with Smith, they would call him. Hardin stepped out of IA office and gave a sigh of relief, thinking that he needed to find Smith and find out where his head was at. He then realized that some of his fellow officers who think like he did were there too. They wanted to know the outcome of the investigation. He told them that they couldn't find anything to hold him on. All they needed to do is speak with Smith now.

He then said, "I don't get it. I don't understand what all the fuss is about. It's just another dead nigger off the streets. One we don't have to worry about out there dealing dope, robbing people, and playing all that dam loud music. Just another dead nigger" and he started to laugh.

CHAPTER 25

HARDIN AND JACKSON'S ENCOUNTER

*A*t that moment, the door opened and in walked Officer Carl Jackson, Jr. He walked in and Hardin turned around to see what the noise was about and he sees Carl, Jr. Hardin tries to read Jackson's face because he knew what he had done to his wife. Jackson walked up to Hardin, nose-to-nose almost.

Officer Hardin asked, "Jackson, what's the problem. I hear you been looking for me."

Jackson told Hardin, "I know the real story about what happened that night."

Everybody was looking at Hardin and listening to Jackson, not understanding where all the animosity between the two came from.

Hardin tells Jackson, "prove it. Sounds like it may be pretty good. But you know what, it's your word against Smith and mine."

"No," Jackson said, "it's going to be your word against Smith and mine."

Hardin said, "What do you mean you and Smith."

Jackson held up Smith's letter, telling Hardin, "Smith wrote to me telling about how you had led him down the wrong path, abused the system, and got away with it. And no, this is not going to be an unhappy ending. This is not going to be one of those situations where everything gets swept under a rug and there is no investigation of the situation to find out what is actually going on."

Jackson continued, "You have the nerve to threaten my

85

wife and child. You let Lil Mike die by not getting medical attention while he was having a seizure."

At that moment, Hardin goes back over that night that Lil Mike died in his thoughts. They had pulled over on the side of the road because Lil Mike was complaining that the handcuffs were on too tight. Lil Mike was shouting profanity to them. "You m----rf-----rs are always tripping. Always f-----g with a Black man cause he's driving a nice ride. Just because he f----d a White b---h and no, I didn't rape her."

At that moment, Hardin pulled Lil Mike out of the back of the car hard and threw him on the ground. Lil Mike's mouth hit a rock and he split his lip.

He tasted the blood, spit it out and said "m----rf-----r take these cuffs off and try that s--t. You punk a-s cops do all your dirt when you have the advantage. Take these cuffs off and try that s--t."

Hardin looked at Lil Mike and smiled. "So you got you some white meat. Did you like it because if your black a-s wasn't who you are with a little money, you'd just be another nigger and she wouldn't have given you the time of day."

Lil Mike said, "f--k you man. You just mad because I hit it and she would never do you."

At that time, Hardin picked him up and threw him hard against the back of the car. Lil Mike groaned and said that he felt sick.

Hardin laughed and said, "so, I'm suppose to believe you now and feel sorry for you."

Lil Mike looked at Smith and said, "I have seizures and I feel one coming on."

Smith said, "that's enough Hardin. We're in enough trouble already. We don't need them looking into this situation too. Lets just get him to the precinct and book him on resisting arrest; and hopefully, they'll believe that's how he got those injuries."

At that moment, Lil Mike went into a grand mal seizure and fell to the ground, jerking back and forth violently.

Smith yelled at Hardin, " help him! Get him up so we can get him to the hospital."

Hardin said, "no" and pushed Smith away from Lil Mike.

Smith said, "he could die; I know because my brother had a big seizure like this. He died because we didn't get him to the hospital in time."

Hardin was still standing between Smith and Lil Mike, he looked at Smith and said, "what's the problem, just another dead nigger, if we're lucky."

Smith was stunned by his words. He pushed Hardin to the side to look at Lil Mike and started trying to get him up to take him to the hospital, but Lil Mike had stopped moving. Smith checked his pulse, turned and looked at Hardin and said, "he's dead."

Hardin said, "and what's the problem?"

At that moment, headlights appeared and a car stopped and Officer Carl Jackson, Jr. stepped out of his car and took in he situation. He ran over to Lil Mike's body, feeling for a pulse, turned and punched Hardin and asked, "what did you do."

Hardin rubbed his jaw and said real calm, "he had a seizure. I didn't kill him. Isn't that right Smith."

Smith looked stunned and said, "yes," but realized how deep of a mess he had gotten himself into. He walked to the back of the car and threw up.

Jackson called for the ambulance then walked over to Hardin and said, "I know you did this. I don't know how we're going to prove you did it."

He turned to Smith and said, "if you know what's good for you, you'll get a new partner."

Smith was still stunned and sick over it all so he just looked at Jackson. Jackson walked back to his car to make a call.

Hardin tells Smith, " pull yourself together. All we have to say is that he had a seizure which is true. We pulled him out of the back seat so he could not hurt himself. But before we could call for help, he died. We were in the process of calling when Jackson showed up."

They heard the sirens from the ambulance getting closer at that moment.

Hardin came back to himself and smiled at Jackson, knowing that the only way Jackson could ever get to the truth was if Smith was to talk.

Hardin and Jackson heard a noise behind them and turned to see what it was. Hardin was looking astonished because it was Steven and Smith walking through the door.

Hardin looked at Smith and said, "what's up man, you missed our meeting with IA. They said they would meet with you later. Everything's okay. Want to go have some coffee or something?"

Smith was looking down at the floor but looked up at Hardin and said, "All I ever wanted was to be a good cop, but I couldn't be one because of you. We could have done a lot of good on the streets if you could have gotten over your prejudice of Blacks. Don't you see it was too easy not to try because that would have meant that you are a loser by your own fault and the Black guy who took your spot on the basketball team was better than you. You didn't want to know it was true or not, you just wanted to hold on to the thought that the Coach just gave it to him because he was Black and not that you just didn't try harder, but thought everything was supposed to be easy because you were white. Maybe he was actually better than you, God forbid. You wouldn't have a reason for living would you?"

Hardin, half laughing said, "where is all this coming from? These niggers put all this in your head," looking at Steven and Jackson.

Smith said, "no. I got it from you. All those talks in the patrol car. I knew it was over when you let that kid die."

Hardin said, "you don't know what you're talking about. He died of a seizure; the medical examiner and the autopsy said so."

"Yes, he did," Smith said, "but we just let him die and did not try to get help for him."

Hardin told Smith, "shut the f--k up. He died because he deserved to die. Some punk kid thinking he's better than me cause he got a little money. He died of a seizure."

"No," Smith said, "we let him die. We could have gotten him to the doctor, but you wouldn't let me."

Hardin knew at that moment Smith had just sealed his faith. Hardin pulled out his weapon and pointed it at Smith, then looked at Jackson, trying to decide which one was the real reason he was in this situation. Not coming to terms that it was his own fault.

The officers pulled out their weapons and told Hardin , "you don't want to do this. We can get you some help."

Hardin kept saying over and over, "I can't go to jail. I can't go to jail." He turned the gun to his head and pulled the trigger. Jackson jumped to stop but it was too late. Hardin looked up at him and smiled and with his last breath said, "Still didn't get me nigger."

Jackson looked at Hardin and said, "Lord, have mercy on his soul."

CHAPTER 26

THE AFTERMATH

(CARL, JR., STEVEN, JAMES,
SEAN/CAPTAIN, WILLIS, & HARDIN)

*I*t has been three years since all of this happened, and the Center is getting ready for its first annual banquet in honor of Lil Mike. Carl, Jr. ended up quitting his job at the police department because of all the attention surrounding Hardin's death and became the Director of Pressures of a Young Black Man. The city seemed to calm down some with regard to police brutality claims. Some of Hardin's buddies are still around bidding their time. As the saying goes, "Rome wasn't built in a day," but with constant education and prayer, most of all, things to come might change with the grace of God.

Jackson is proud of how much of a difference the Center has made and how people are thinking more about each other than themselves. But you know, just like 9-11, we were one for a minute, but then when it got old, old prejudices came back. But God has the last say-so on everything.

Steven Young has taken a position in the District Attorney's office. He thinks that by being on the inside, he may be able to make a difference in how the District Attorney's office looks at Blacks and pray everything stays honest. You know the saying, "In God We Trust."

James Benton still does not understand why he didn't get the manager's job, but his wife had said at the time what God has for you, it's for you. James was called to the corporate office for a meeting and he was asked to bring his wife. Not knowing what was going on, they went. When they got there, they met with the CEO and board members. They showed him a trend line of the company's sales and his store sales when he was in charge. The graph showed his store sales were well above everyone elses. They told him that he had set records unknown till now and that they understood that he may have felt slighted by the manager's position being given to someone else. But they couldn't discuss it with him at the time because of not having the board's approval. Now that they had it, they wanted to offer him a new position that was created for him - VP of Store Operation for Sales Building.

James stopped breathing. His wife said, "Thank you Jesus. Thank you Jesus."

When he was finally able to say something, he told them that he accepted the position and that his wife had told him when he didn't get the manager's position that she couldn't wait to see what God had in store for him. They told him he that he deserved it and he didn't have to move but can work out of his home but he would do a lot of traveling and that his wife would be allowed to accompany him.

James and his wife went back to the hotel in tears in the back of the cab, thanking God. The cab driver looked at them and said, "God is good all the time. And when he shows up, he shows out." They all smiled and nodded their heads in agreement that God is good all the time.

Smooth's luck seemed to have run out. He had been caught by Captain's men and they were bringing him back. When they got to where they were supposed to meet Captain, he told the other guys to go, he wanted to do this one himself. When they left, Smooth started trying to explain, saying he knew that what he did was not "what it do." But they left him no choice. He was caught between a rock and a hard place with nowhere to run, so he turned state. He said he knew that "when you live

91

by the code, you die by the code" because he knew he broke it.

Captain looked at Smooth and said, "I don't blame you because if I was in your shoes, I would have done the same thing. The game done changed and if you don't change with the game, you are lost. That was my first and last mistake, getting that close to the product. I'm out, going to work for my father's company. I've got the skills. How do you think I ran this block for so long without getting caught? Man change your life. Take this money and stay clean. Use it as an investment. You know how you love rebuilding cars. Put that talent to good use. Like Puff Daddy says, "Lets do the damn thing"; and God be with you always."

Captain continued, "this is me man, you are not the first one to disappear without a trace. Just hit me in the back of the head and leave me here; they will come back and find me. We are done. I love you man."

Smooth said,"man, you got me crying. This is not what it do."

Captain looked at him and said, "yes it is." Smooth hit Captain over the had and left, taking the money.

He started his own custom body shop and is doing well, still not slinging drugs. He got married and has a beautiful daughter. He told his wife the whole story about his past, about how he was given a second chance in life by Sean, but most of all, by God. And in his nightly prayer, he thanks God for Captain/Sean. He goes to church now and became a member of the Big Brothers so he could help someone else, and hopefully can change another life.

Captain/Sean came to when they came looking for him. They asked if he wanted them to go and find Smooth again; Captain said no. He said this is a sign for him to get out of the game. They looked at him like he was crazy. They asked about the money. He said "it's yours." When God tells you its time, its time.

Always be in tune to Him. They looked at him and said, "what you know about God? You got us out here slinging drugs every day."

Sean said, "your path here on this earth was already drawn and sometimes we make a wrong turn. If I was not supposed to be here, I wouldn't be telling you this now." He turned and walked away from them. Then turned back with a smile on his face and said "When God talks, make sure you're listening."

Sean went to work for his father. He told his father the whole story that even though he had a great life without having to want for anything, it was provisions without nurturing. Even though we had everything, all we wanted was his parents' time.

His father said through his tears, "I know my son. The Lord has fixed it so we can have this time until he says otherwise and take one of us home. He knows our heart and he hears our prayers. This is my gift from God, my son home."

Sean worked himself up through the ranks and earned, not given, the position of his father's right hand. He asked his father to do one thing for him, look at a promoting young man by the name of Willis. He explained his situation. His father stated he does not do favors. If the young man does a good job, then he doesn't have a problem with it. Sean said, "thanks dad."

Sean is still not married, but has been called to preach.

Willis got a memo to go to personnel. He walked slowly thinking he was being fired. Even though Sean took care of all the legal fees and he only lost one day of work, he was still struggling to make ends meet and take care of his girls. When he reached the door, he said a little prayer. "Whatever your will Lord, just make me strong enough to go through it." He walked in and the personnel manager was in his secretary's office waiting on him, looking over his job performance. He told Willis that someone recommended him for the position of Supervisor over the day shift. This position comes with all the benefits (medical, dental, life, bonus, plus three weeks vacation). Willis thought his heart was going to burst through his chest. He was so excited and could not thank the personnel manager enough, and Jesus. He asked who had recommended him. The manager told him he could not say, but if his work standards were not what they were, he would not have gotten the job, even if the President had recommended him himself.

Willis read through the lines, saying thank you a couple more times and left the office. He was walking down the hallway about to burst and bumped into Sean.

Sean explained, "I've been here six months already." He looked at Willis and said, "you look like you got some good news."

Willis stated, "yeah man. I did and God knows I needed it."

Sean looked at him and said, "I know," and walked off.

As Sean walked off, Willis said, "thank you Lord for a friend like Sean. And for always being there for him and his family." He knows that God doesn't make mistakes. That's how he got over the lost of his wife. He had prayed for God not to take her this last time and God spoke to him and told him if he took her he would get to see her again.

CHAPTER 27

AMBER

*A*mber could not believe that she could have sank so low that she accused someone of rape when he didn't do it and the bruises she done to herself. She was just coming to terms with all that. It took a while for the doctor to even get her to talk, during the first year she was admitted.

She always talked about how Lil Mike loved her and only wanted her one minute; then the next, in a fit of tears, talks about how she lied and didn't mean to hurt anyone.

She was sorry, so very sorry, she didn't mean to hurt him. She came a long way, but she got a long road ahead of her too. The nightmare comes less now with it being three years behind her. She is conscious of certain things.

She always has a Bible folded up in her arms. Some of the nurses aides tease and joke, saying that she started to make progress when she started holding on to God's words.

CHAPTER 28

T-MAX

T-max is still playing with the NFL, setting all kinds of records. He even has been to the pro bowl the last three years.

On the off season, he works with the Center at least three days a week. He has a summer camp that he paid for and takes 20 boys to one home game every year and pays for it. All of this is his way of giving back to the community.

He does not dwell upon being adopted anymore. He came to an understanding when he met Lil Mike that it could have been worst. Suppose his mother had abandoned him as Lil Mike's mother had and he would have been a ward of the State, passed around from foster home to foster home.

T-max gave thanks to God everyday for his real mother and his adopted parents. He's still not married, but dating someone seriously.

CHAPTER 29

JOHN SMITH

*J*ohn Smith has paid his debt through the legal system, and now, he goes around the country talking about police brutality not being reported by fellow officers and how the interaction with the cops can change some situations. He is not real popular with the police departments because he exposes some of their secrets. He has gotten death threats because of it. And he thanks God for giving him another chance and this is why he can still go on. He works for Pressures of a Young Black Man and the lectures are set up through the Center. "Who would have thought?" God has a purpose for every one.

The fundraiser for the Center was going to be a great success. Steven gave the history of the Center and why it was established. Why its an honor to dedicate the first one in memory of Michael Edwards, aka Lil Mike.

Randy finished what Lil Mike had started with Tristen and his group. He took them to the record company and they signed on the spot. They all miss Lil Mike, but know he would be proud of them. They have recorded a song called "Pressures of a Black Man" in honor of the Center and will donate a percentage of the profits to the Center. They are going to perform it for the first time at the fundraiser that night. Everything is better than they could have ever imagined.

Steven and Carl, Jr. are in rare form. T-max flew in for the event. James, Sean, and Willis are there, along with the other volunteers. All of the City Officials are there too. Steven and Carl, Jr. got some good news. The Mayor told them that their Center had been named to be the new prototype because of their success with the Center. The government wants to try and duplicate the system which works to bridge the gap between the police department and the community they serve.

Steven and Carl, Jr. were sitting and talking about the night's events and everything that had happened.

Carl, Jr. tells Steven, "this proves that everything we do in life, God has control of."

Steven said, "there's no doubt about it."

THE END

R. M. Brown

Born in Monroe, Louisiana, she is a U. S. Army veteran. She always believes in God's favor. Although never intending to be a published author, she is thrilled to see God's favor come full circle in her life. A special thanks to Re-Al who inspired her to write this book with his special song, "Pressures of a Young Black Man." She is a mother of two daughters, Lamica Nicole Brown and Krystal Nicole Brown. She is married to a wonderful man, Michael R. Bell, who was sent by God.